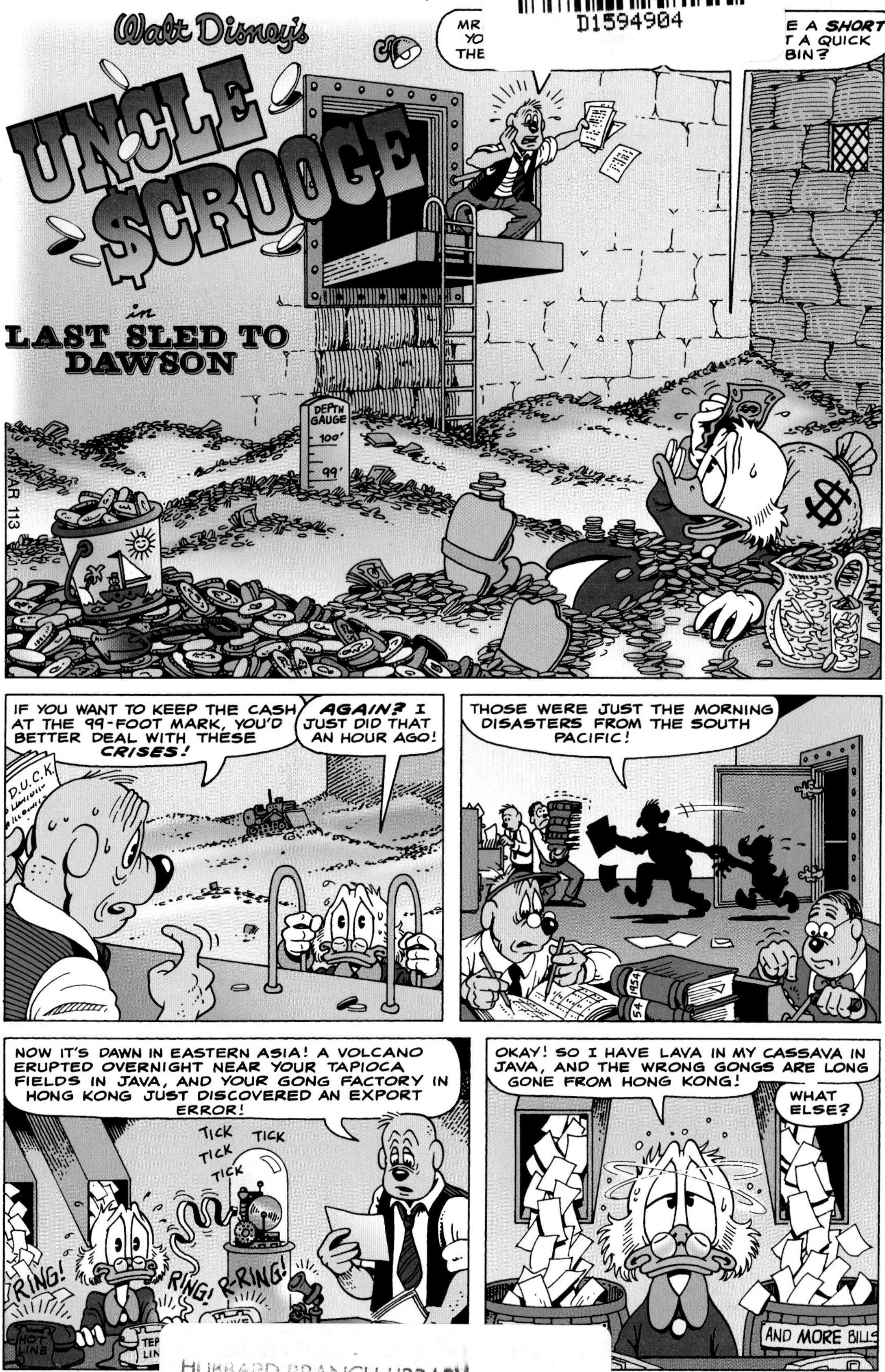
Walt Disney's
UNCLE $CROOGE
in
LAST SLED TO DAWSON
DEPTH GAUGE
100'
99'
AR 113
IF YOU WANT TO KEEP THE CASH AT THE 99-FOOT MARK, YOU'D BETTER DEAL WITH THESE CRISES!
AGAIN? I JUST DID THAT AN HOUR AGO!
D.U.C.K.
THOSE WERE JUST THE MORNING DISASTERS FROM THE SOUTH PACIFIC!
1954
54
NOW IT'S DAWN IN EASTERN ASIA! A VOLCANO ERUPTED OVERNIGHT NEAR YOUR TAPIOCA FIELDS IN JAVA, AND YOUR GONG FACTORY IN HONG KONG JUST DISCOVERED AN EXPORT ERROR!
TICK TICK TICK TICK
RING! RING! R-RING!
HOT LINE
OKAY! SO I HAVE LAVA IN MY CASSAVA IN JAVA, AND THE WRONG GONGS ARE LONG GONE FROM HONG KONG!
WHAT ELSE?
AND MORE BILLS

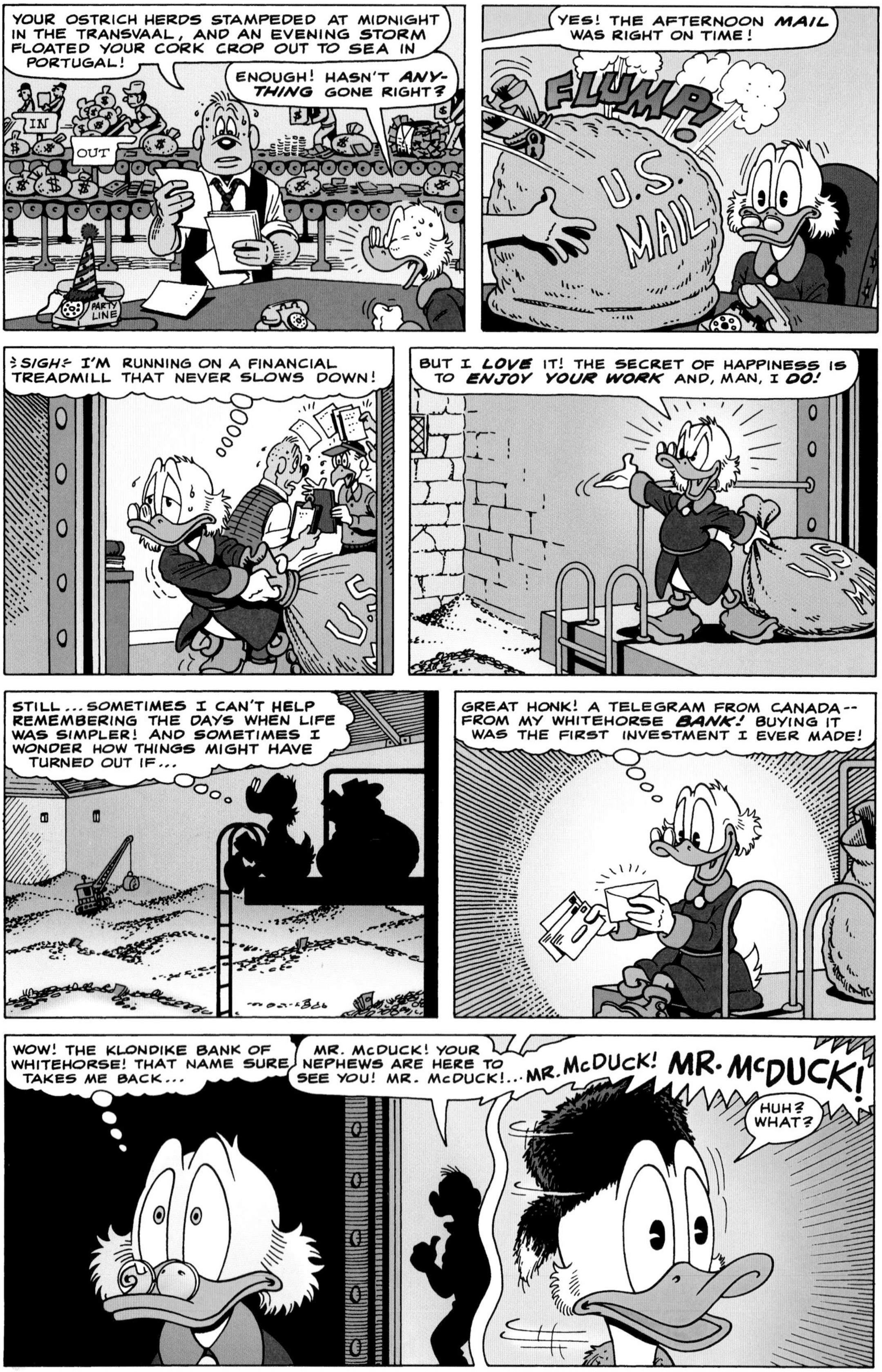
YOUR OSTRICH HERDS STAMPEDED AT MIDNIGHT IN THE TRANSVAAL, AND AN EVENING STORM FLOATED YOUR CORK CROP OUT TO SEA IN PORTUGAL!
IN
OUT
PARTY LINE
ENOUGH! HASN'T ANYTHING GONE RIGHT?
YES! THE AFTERNOON MAIL WAS RIGHT ON TIME!
FLUMP!
U.S. MAIL
-SIGH- I'M RUNNING ON A FINANCIAL TREADMILL THAT NEVER SLOWS DOWN!
BUT I LOVE IT! THE SECRET OF HAPPINESS IS TO ENJOY YOUR WORK AND, MAN, I DO!
STILL... SOMETIMES I CAN'T HELP REMEMBERING THE DAYS WHEN LIFE WAS SIMPLER! AND SOMETIMES I WONDER HOW THINGS MIGHT HAVE TURNED OUT IF...
GREAT HONK! A TELEGRAM FROM CANADA-- FROM MY WHITEHORSE BANK! BUYING IT WAS THE FIRST INVESTMENT I EVER MADE!
WOW! THE KLONDIKE BANK OF WHITEHORSE! THAT NAME SURE TAKES ME BACK...
MR. McDUCK! YOUR NEPHEWS ARE HERE TO SEE YOU! MR. McDUCK!... MR. McDUCK! MR. McDUCK!
HUH? WHAT?

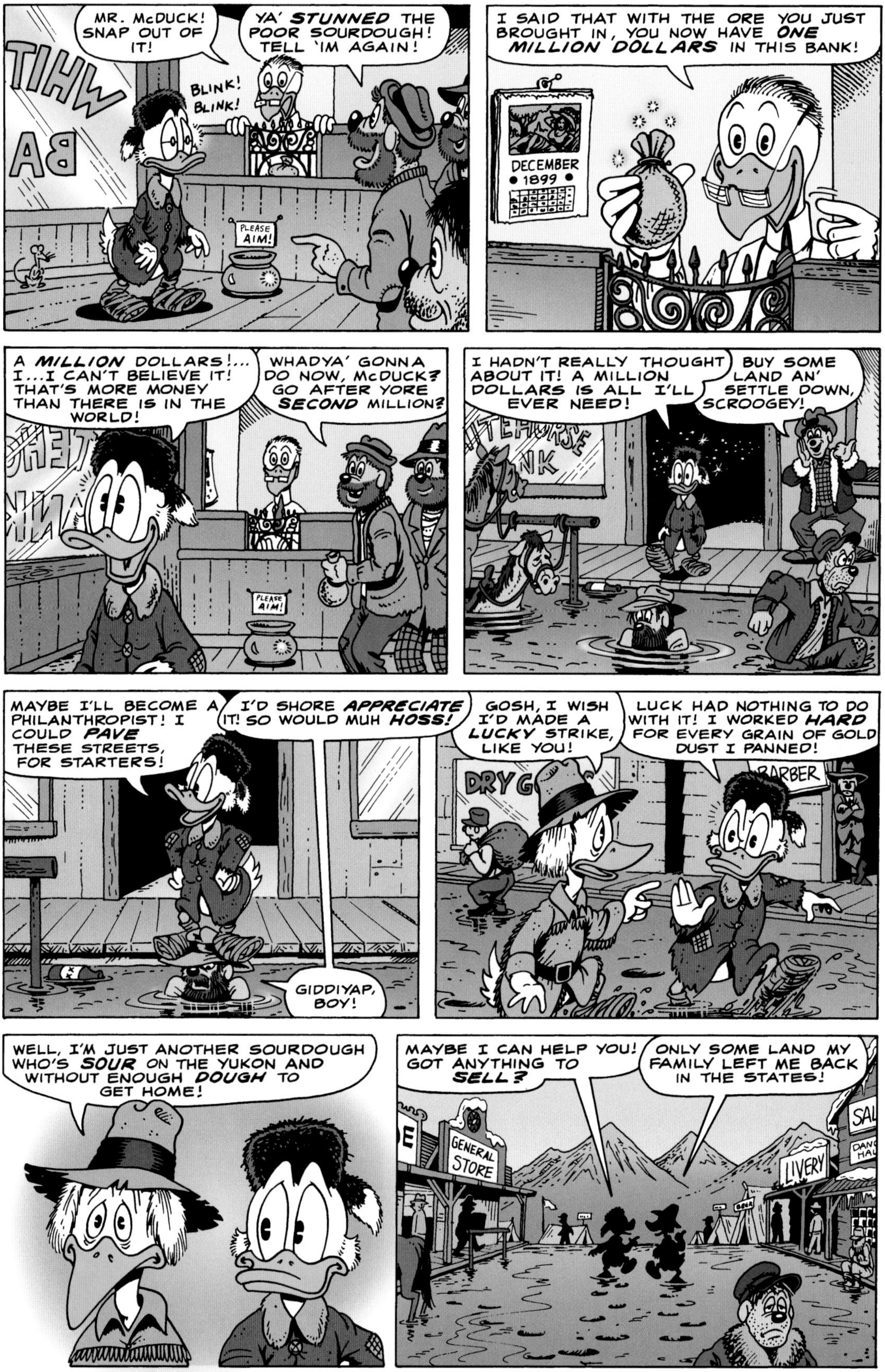

MR. McDUCK! SNAP OUT OF IT!
YA' STUNNED THE POOR SOURDOUGH! TELL 'IM AGAIN!
BLINK! BLINK!
WHIT
BA
PLEASE AIM!
I SAID THAT WITH THE ORE YOU JUST BROUGHT IN, YOU NOW HAVE ONE MILLION DOLLARS IN THIS BANK!
DECEMBER 1899
A MILLION DOLLARS!... I...I CAN'T BELIEVE IT! THAT'S MORE MONEY THAN THERE IS IN THE WORLD!
WHADYA' GONNA DO NOW, McDUCK? GO AFTER YORE SECOND MILLION?
PLEASE AIM!
I HADN'T REALLY THOUGHT ABOUT IT! A MILLION DOLLARS IS ALL I'LL EVER NEED!
BUY SOME LAND AN' SETTLE DOWN, SCROOGEY!
NK
MAYBE I'LL BECOME A PHILANTHROPIST! I COULD PAVE THESE STREETS, FOR STARTERS!
I'D SHORE APPRECIATE IT! SO WOULD MUH HOSS!
GIDDIYAP, BOY!
GOSH, I WISH I'D MADE A LUCKY STRIKE, LIKE YOU!
LUCK HAD NOTHING TO DO WITH IT! I WORKED HARD FOR EVERY GRAIN OF GOLD DUST I PANNED!
DRY G
BARBER
WELL, I'M JUST ANOTHER SOURDOUGH WHO'S SOUR ON THE YUKON AND WITHOUT ENOUGH DOUGH TO GET HOME!
MAYBE I CAN HELP YOU! GOT ANYTHING TO SELL?
ONLY SOME LAND MY FAMILY LEFT ME BACK IN THE STATES!
GENERAL STORE
LIVERY

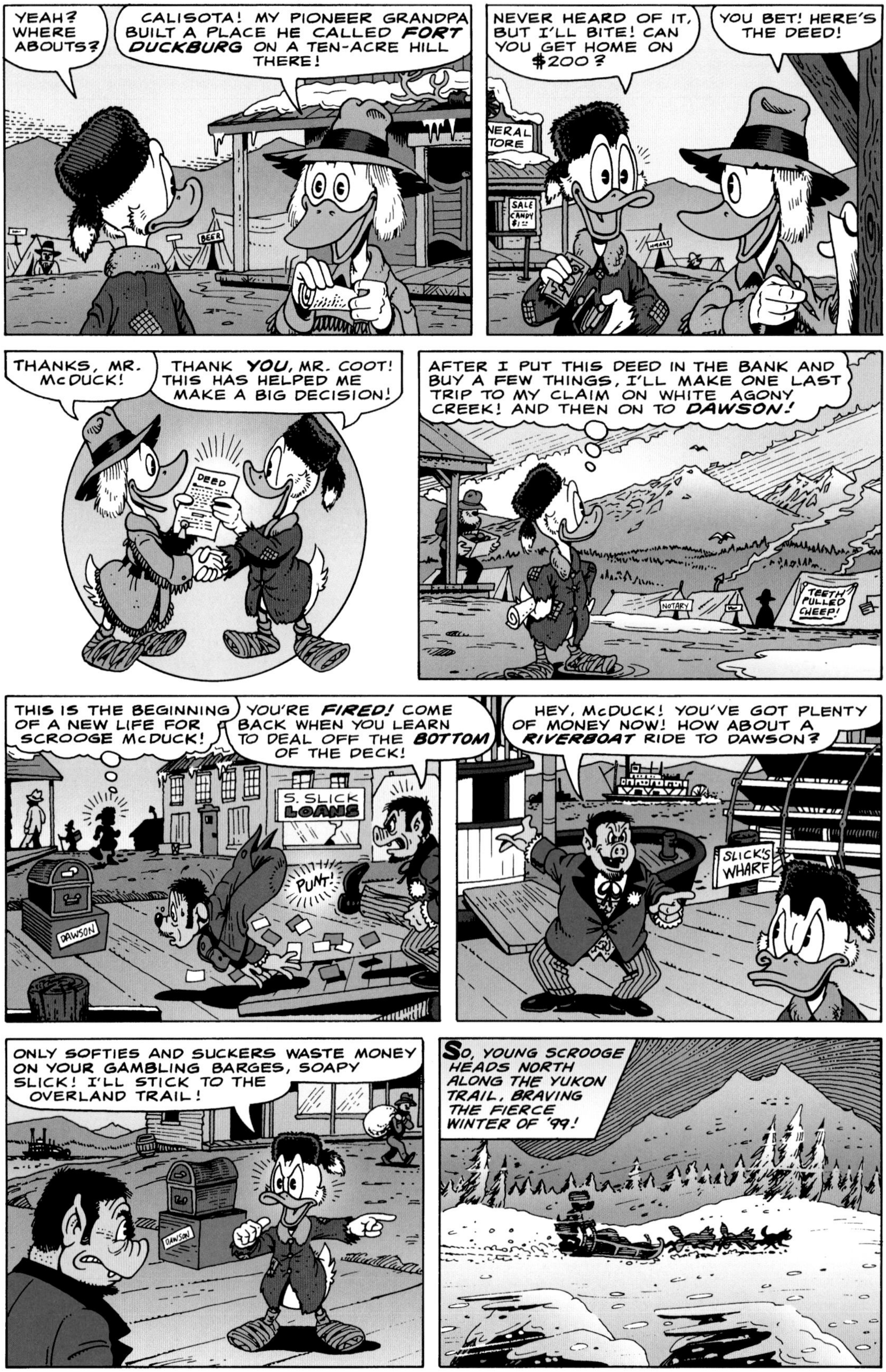
YEAH? WHERE ABOUTS?
CALISOTA! MY PIONEER GRANDPA BUILT A PLACE HE CALLED FORT DUCKBURG ON A TEN-ACRE HILL THERE!
BEER
NEVER HEARD OF IT, BUT I'LL BITE! CAN YOU GET HOME ON $200?
YOU BET! HERE'S THE DEED!
SALE CANDY $1
THANKS, MR. McDUCK!
THANK YOU, MR. COOT! THIS HAS HELPED ME MAKE A BIG DECISION!
DEED
AFTER I PUT THIS DEED IN THE BANK AND BUY A FEW THINGS, I'LL MAKE ONE LAST TRIP TO MY CLAIM ON WHITE AGONY CREEK! AND THEN ON TO DAWSON!
NOTARY
TEETH PULLED CHEEP!
THIS IS THE BEGINNING OF A NEW LIFE FOR SCROOGE McDUCK!
YOU'RE FIRED! COME BACK WHEN YOU LEARN TO DEAL OFF THE BOTTOM OF THE DECK!
S. SLICK LOANS
PUNT!
DAWSON
HEY, McDUCK! YOU'VE GOT PLENTY OF MONEY NOW! HOW ABOUT A RIVERBOAT RIDE TO DAWSON?
SLICK'S WHARF
ONLY SOFTIES AND SUCKERS WASTE MONEY ON YOUR GAMBLING BARGES, SOAPY SLICK! I'LL STICK TO THE OVERLAND TRAIL!
DAWSON
SO, YOUNG SCROOGE HEADS NORTH ALONG THE YUKON TRAIL, BRAVING THE FIERCE WINTER OF '99!

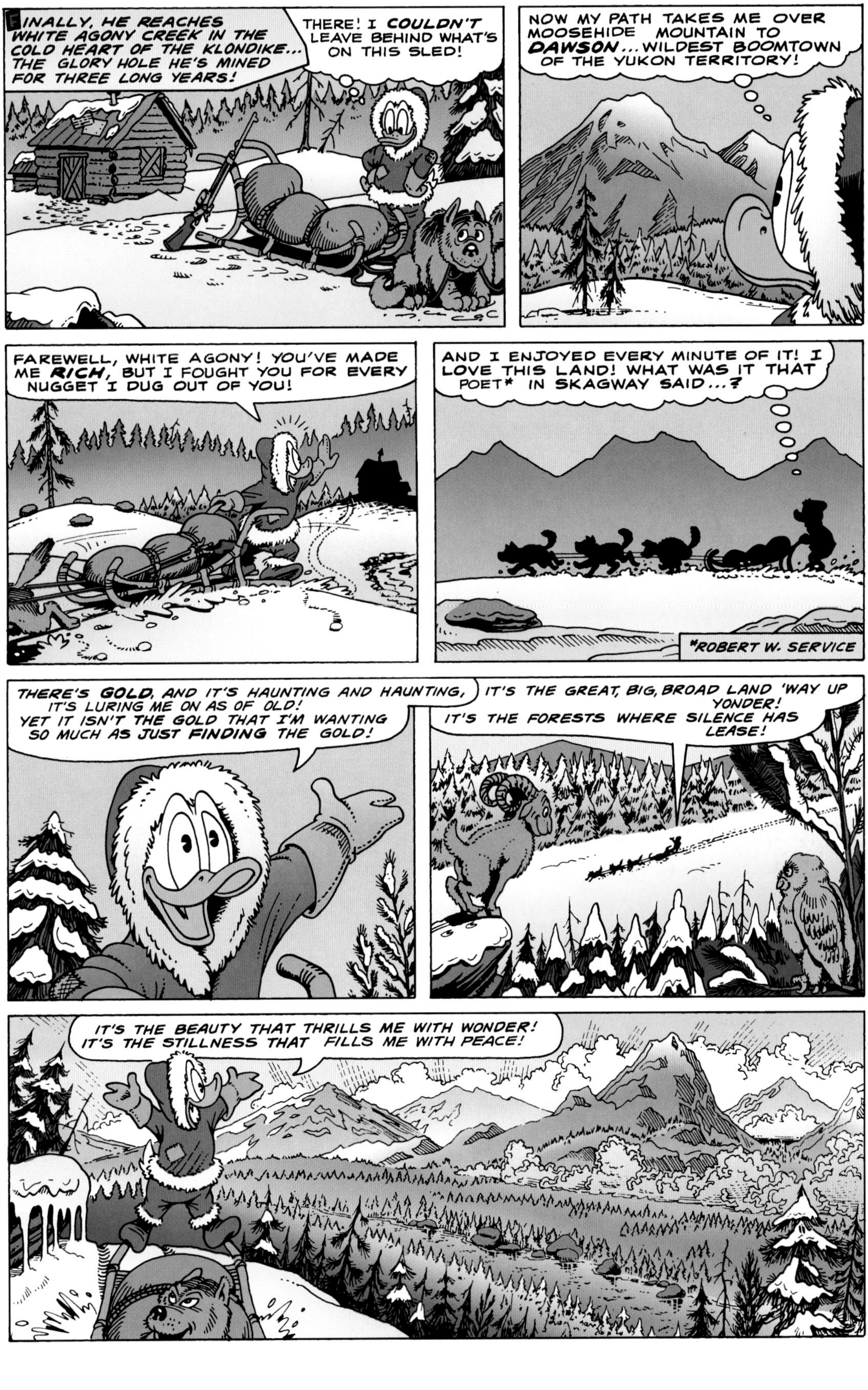
FINALLY, HE REACHES WHITE AGONY CREEK IN THE COLD HEART OF THE KLONDIKE... THE GLORY HOLE HE'S MINED FOR THREE LONG YEARS!
THERE! I COULDN'T LEAVE BEHIND WHAT'S ON THIS SLED!
NOW MY PATH TAKES ME OVER MOOSEHIDE MOUNTAIN TO DAWSON... WILDEST BOOMTOWN OF THE YUKON TERRITORY!
FAREWELL, WHITE AGONY! YOU'VE MADE ME RICH, BUT I FOUGHT YOU FOR EVERY NUGGET I DUG OUT OF YOU!
AND I ENJOYED EVERY MINUTE OF IT! I LOVE THIS LAND! WHAT WAS IT THAT POET* IN SKAGWAY SAID...?
*ROBERT W. SERVICE
THERE'S GOLD, AND IT'S HAUNTING AND HAUNTING, IT'S LURING ME ON AS OF OLD! YET IT ISN'T THE GOLD THAT I'M WANTING SO MUCH AS JUST FINDING THE GOLD!
IT'S THE GREAT, BIG, BROAD LAND 'WAY UP YONDER! IT'S THE FORESTS WHERE SILENCE HAS LEASE!
IT'S THE BEAUTY THAT THRILLS ME WITH WONDER! IT'S THE STILLNESS THAT FILLS ME WITH PEACE!

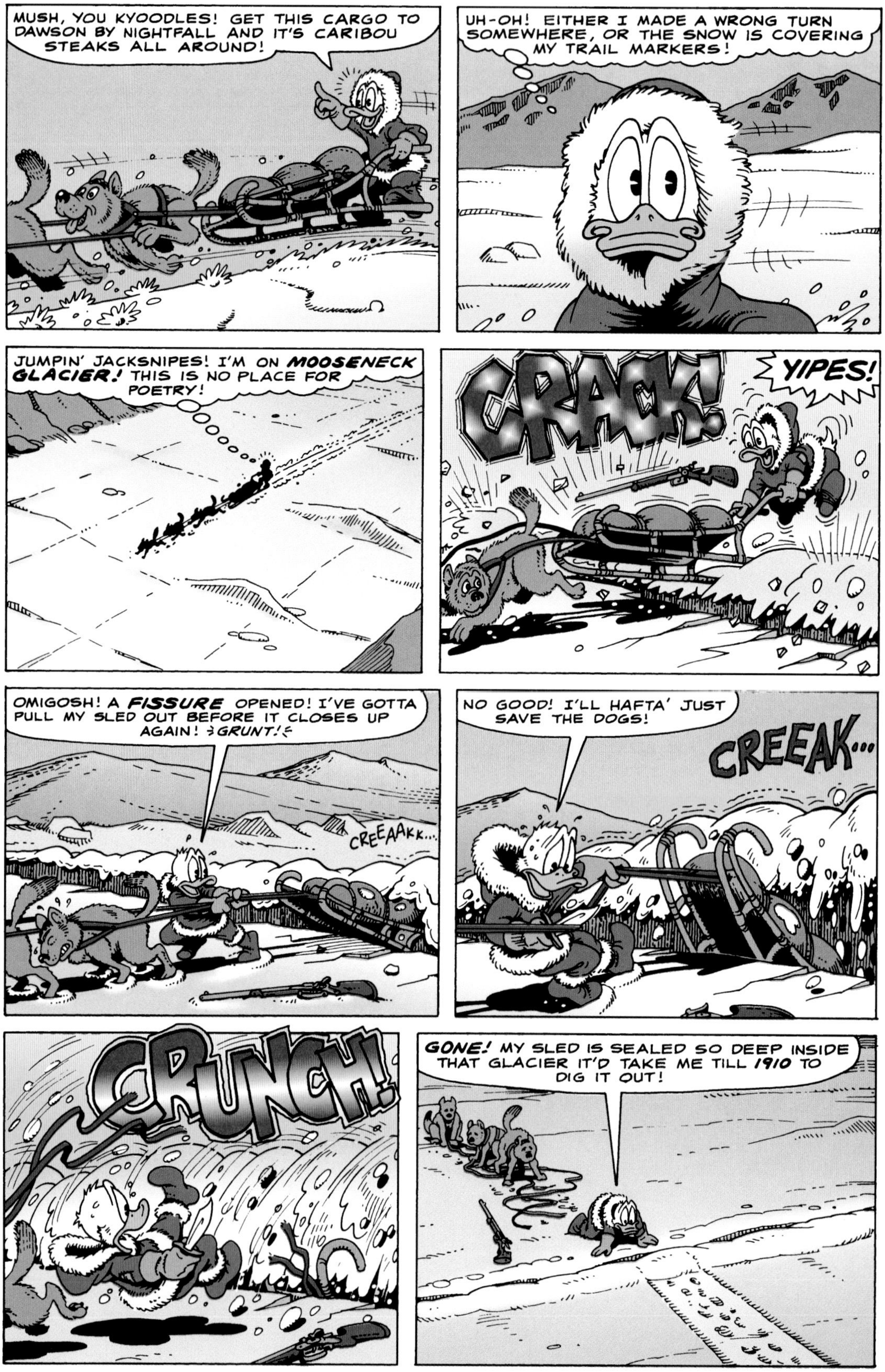

MUSH, YOU KYOODLES! GET THIS CARGO TO DAWSON BY NIGHTFALL AND IT'S CARIBOU STEAKS ALL AROUND!
UH-OH! EITHER I MADE A WRONG TURN SOMEWHERE, OR THE SNOW IS COVERING MY TRAIL MARKERS!
JUMPIN' JACKSNIPES! I'M ON MOOSENECK GLACIER! THIS IS NO PLACE FOR POETRY!
CRACK!
YIPES!
OMIGOSH! A FISSURE OPENED! I'VE GOTTA PULL MY SLED OUT BEFORE IT CLOSES UP AGAIN! GRUNT!
CREEAAKK...
NO GOOD! I'LL HAFTA' JUST SAVE THE DOGS!
CREEAK...
CRUNCH!
GONE! MY SLED IS SEALED SO DEEP INSIDE THAT GLACIER IT'D TAKE ME TILL 1910 TO DIG IT OUT!

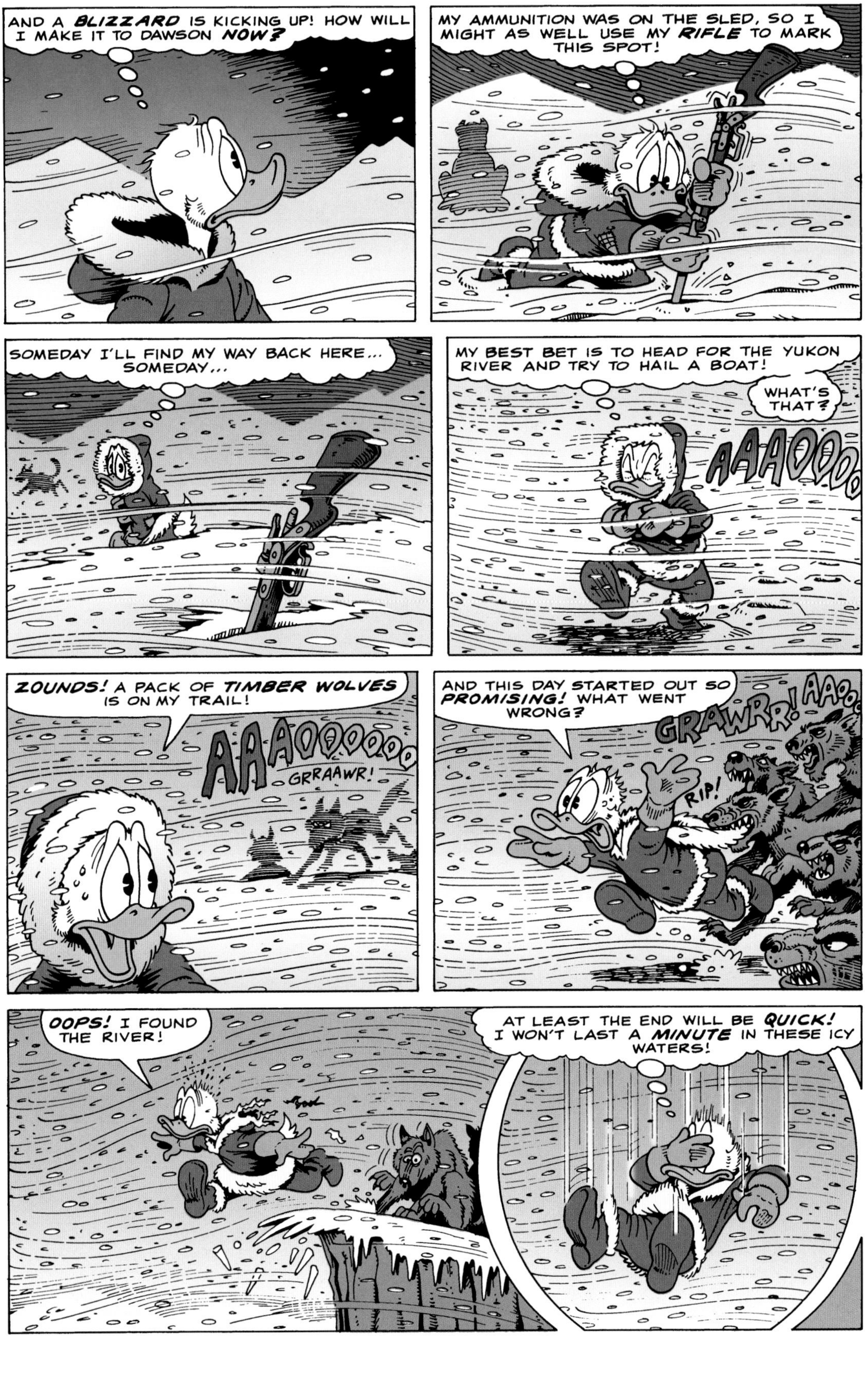
AND A BLIZZARD IS KICKING UP! HOW WILL I MAKE IT TO DAWSON NOW?
MY AMMUNITION WAS ON THE SLED, SO I MIGHT AS WELL USE MY RIFLE TO MARK THIS SPOT!
SOMEDAY I'LL FIND MY WAY BACK HERE... SOMEDAY...
MY BEST BET IS TO HEAD FOR THE YUKON RIVER AND TRY TO HAIL A BOAT!
WHAT'S THAT?
AAAOOOO
ZOUNDS! A PACK OF TIMBER WOLVES IS ON MY TRAIL!
AAAOOOOOOO
GRRAAWR!
AND THIS DAY STARTED OUT SO PROMISING! WHAT WENT WRONG?
GRAWRR! AAO
RIP!
OOPS! I FOUND THE RIVER!
AT LEAST THE END WILL BE QUICK! I WON'T LAST A MINUTE IN THESE ICY WATERS!

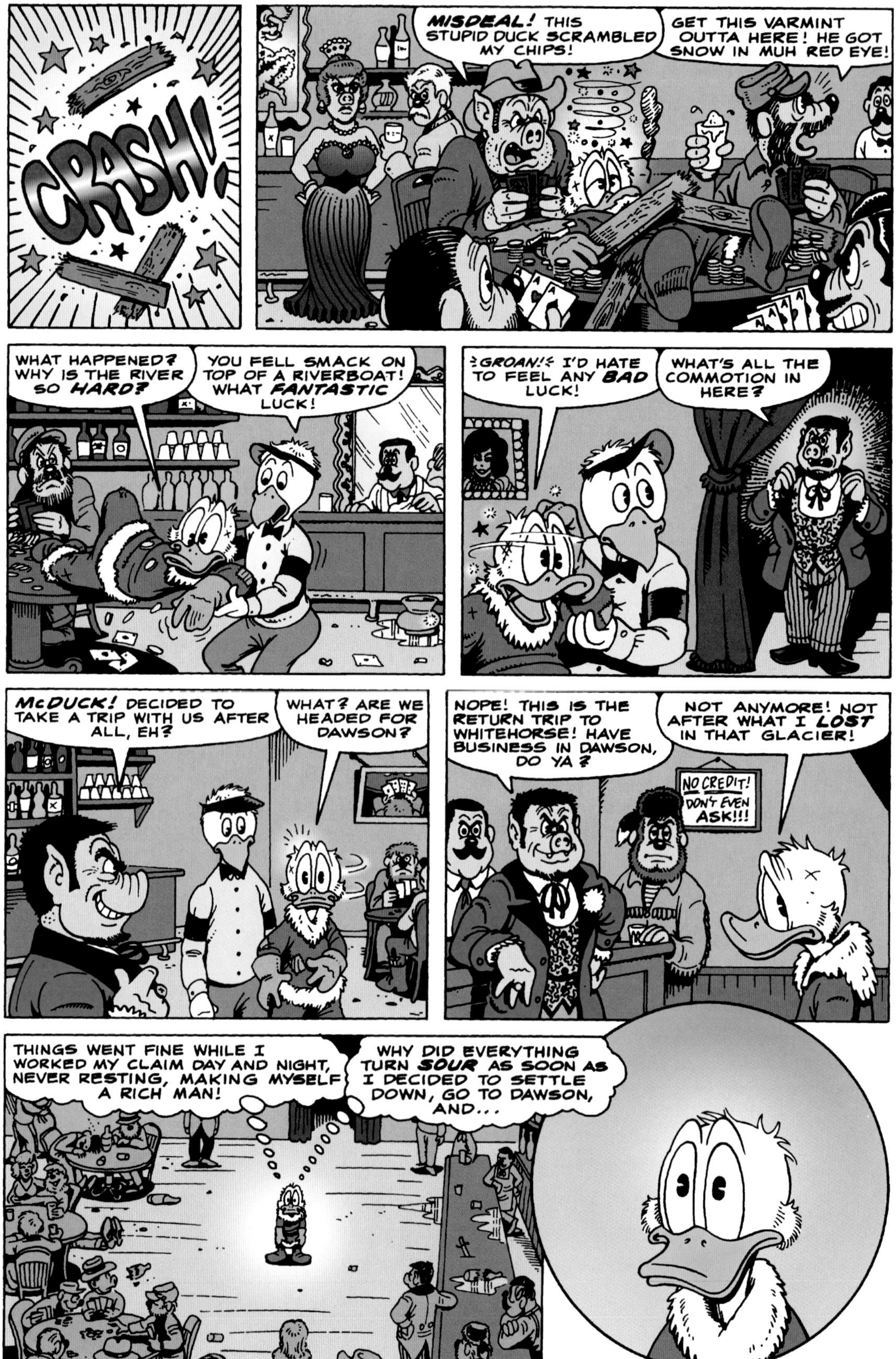
CRASH!
MISDEAL! THIS STUPID DUCK SCRAMBLED MY CHIPS!
GET THIS VARMINT OUTTA HERE! HE GOT SNOW IN MUH RED EYE!
WHAT HAPPENED? WHY IS THE RIVER SO HARD?
YOU FELL SMACK ON TOP OF A RIVERBOAT! WHAT FANTASTIC LUCK!
GROAN! I'D HATE TO FEEL ANY BAD LUCK!
WHAT'S ALL THE COMMOTION IN HERE?
McDUCK! DECIDED TO TAKE A TRIP WITH US AFTER ALL, EH?
WHAT? ARE WE HEADED FOR DAWSON?
NOPE! THIS IS THE RETURN TRIP TO WHITEHORSE! HAVE BUSINESS IN DAWSON, DO YA?
NOT ANYMORE! NOT AFTER WHAT I LOST IN THAT GLACIER!
NO CREDIT! DON'T EVEN ASK!!!
THINGS WENT FINE WHILE I WORKED MY CLAIM DAY AND NIGHT, NEVER RESTING, MAKING MYSELF A RICH MAN!
WHY DID EVERYTHING TURN SOUR AS SOON AS I DECIDED TO SETTLE DOWN, GO TO DAWSON, AND...

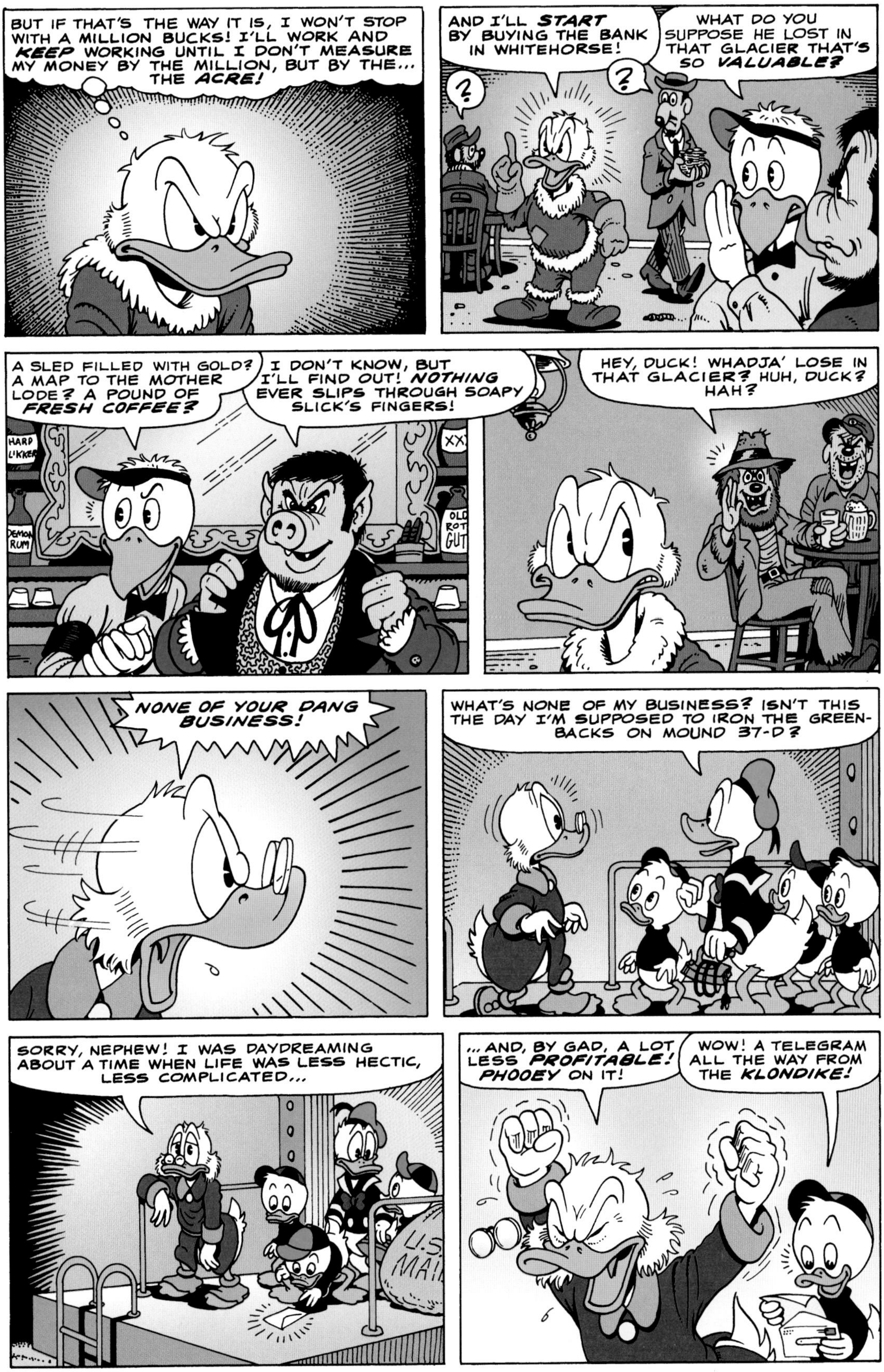
BUT IF THAT'S THE WAY IT IS, I WON'T STOP WITH A MILLION BUCKS! I'LL WORK AND KEEP WORKING UNTIL I DON'T MEASURE MY MONEY BY THE MILLION, BUT BY THE... THE ACRE!
AND I'LL START BY BUYING THE BANK IN WHITEHORSE!
?
?
WHAT DO YOU SUPPOSE HE LOST IN THAT GLACIER THAT'S SO VALUABLE?
A SLED FILLED WITH GOLD? A MAP TO THE MOTHER LODE? A POUND OF FRESH COFFEE?
I DON'T KNOW, BUT I'LL FIND OUT! NOTHING EVER SLIPS THROUGH SOAPY SLICK'S FINGERS!
HARD L'IKKER
DEMON RUM
OLD ROT GUT
HEY, DUCK! WHADJA' LOSE IN THAT GLACIER? HUH, DUCK? HAH?
NONE OF YOUR DANG BUSINESS!
WHAT'S NONE OF MY BUSINESS? ISN'T THIS THE DAY I'M SUPPOSED TO IRON THE GREEN-BACKS ON MOUND 37-D?
SORRY, NEPHEW! I WAS DAYDREAMING ABOUT A TIME WHEN LIFE WAS LESS HECTIC, LESS COMPLICATED...
...AND, BY GAD, A LOT LESS PROFITABLE! PHOOEY ON IT!
WOW! A TELEGRAM ALL THE WAY FROM THE KLONDIKE!

IT'S FROM YOUR WHITEHORSE BANK, UNCA SCROOGE!

SO WHAT?! THAT BANK HAS BEEN A WHITE *ELEPHANT* SINCE THE GOLD FIELDS PLAYED OUT!

THEY SAY YOU LEFT STANDING ORDERS TO KEEP TABS ON SOME MARKER IN A GLACIER!

AND THE MARKER AREA IS ABOUT TO FALL INTO THE YUKON RIVER!

MY MARKER? MOOSENECK GLACIER? OH, MY HEAVENLY DAYS! I'VE BEEN WAITING FOR THIS MOMENT FOR *YEARS!*

GLOM!

WHIT!

DIG OUT YOUR OVERCOATS AND PACK YOUR BAGS, BOYS!

WE'RE GOING BACK TO THE KLONDIKE... *AGAIN!!!*

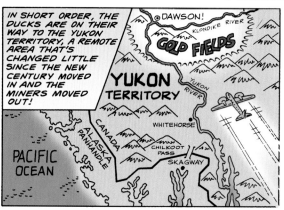

IN SHORT ORDER, THE DUCKS ARE ON THEIR WAY TO THE YUKON TERRITORY, A REMOTE AREA THAT'S CHANGED LITTLE SINCE THE NEW CENTURY MOVED IN AND THE MINERS MOVED OUT!

DAWSON!

KLONDIKE RIVER

GOLD FIELDS

YUKON TERRITORY

YUKON RIVER

WHITEHORSE

CHILKOOT PASS

SKAGWAY

ALASKA PANHANDLE

CANADA

PACIFIC OCEAN

HERE IT IS, UNCA SCROOGE! A GLACIER FORMS WHEN SNOW ON A MOUNTAIN NEVER GETS WARM ENOUGH TO MELT! THE COMPACTED MASS MOVES *SLOWLY,* LIKE A SOLID RIVER, A FEW FEET EACH YEAR!

Z

YES, BOYS...

...THAT'S WHY I HAD THE BANK KEEP AN EYE ON MY MARKER! WHEN MY CHUNK FALLS INTO THE RIVER I'LL *FINALLY* BE ABLE TO RETRIEVE MY DOGSLED!

DAWSON, Y.T.

RAMJET FLYING SER

GOSH, UNCLE SCROOGE! WHAT'S ON THE SLED THAT'S SO IMPORTANT?

NOTHING THAT CONCERNS YOU! YOU GET 30 CENTS AN HOUR TO HELP ME, NOT TO BE SO DANG *NOSEY!*

RAMJET, I A DIV. OF McDUCK IN

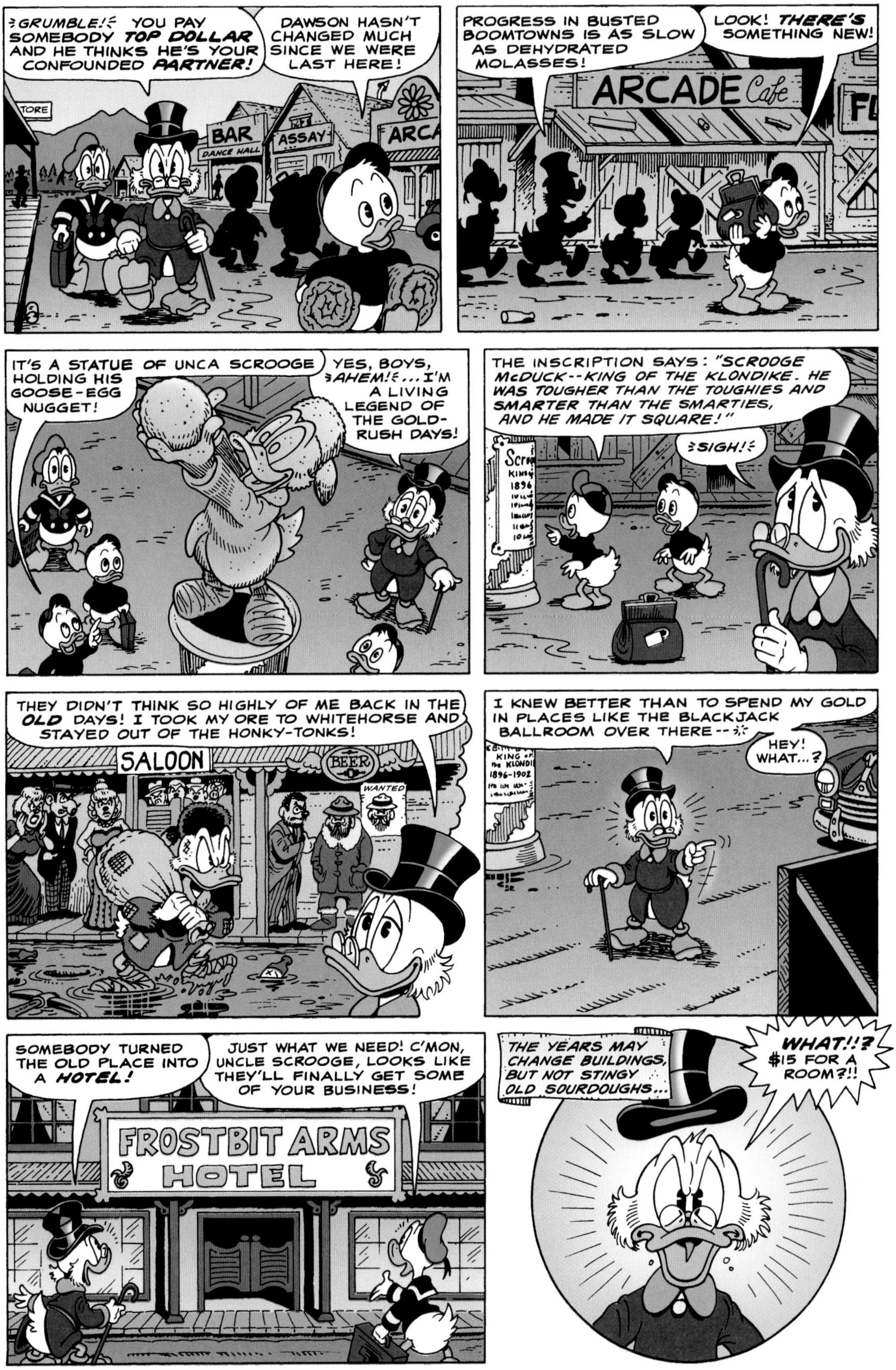
⁝GRUMBLE!⁝ YOU PAY SOMEBODY TOP DOLLAR AND HE THINKS HE'S YOUR CONFOUNDED PARTNER!
DAWSON HASN'T CHANGED MUCH SINCE WE WERE LAST HERE!
BAR
DANCE HALL
ASSAY
PROGRESS IN BUSTED BOOMTOWNS IS AS SLOW AS DEHYDRATED MOLASSES!
LOOK! THERE'S SOMETHING NEW!
ARCADE Cafe
IT'S A STATUE OF UNCA SCROOGE HOLDING HIS GOOSE-EGG NUGGET!
YES, BOYS, ⁝AHEM!⁝... I'M A LIVING LEGEND OF THE GOLD-RUSH DAYS!
THE INSCRIPTION SAYS: "SCROOGE McDUCK--KING OF THE KLONDIKE. HE WAS TOUGHER THAN THE TOUGHIES AND SMARTER THAN THE SMARTIES, AND HE MADE IT SQUARE!"
⁝SIGH!⁝
THEY DIDN'T THINK SO HIGHLY OF ME BACK IN THE OLD DAYS! I TOOK MY ORE TO WHITEHORSE AND STAYED OUT OF THE HONKY-TONKS!
SALOON
BEER
WANTED
I KNEW BETTER THAN TO SPEND MY GOLD IN PLACES LIKE THE BLACKJACK BALLROOM OVER THERE--
HEY! WHAT...?
SOMEBODY TURNED THE OLD PLACE INTO A HOTEL!
JUST WHAT WE NEED! C'MON, UNCLE SCROOGE, LOOKS LIKE THEY'LL FINALLY GET SOME OF YOUR BUSINESS!
FROSTBIT ARMS HOTEL
THE YEARS MAY CHANGE BUILDINGS, BUT NOT STINGY OLD SOURDOUGHS...
WHAT!!? $15 FOR A ROOM?!!

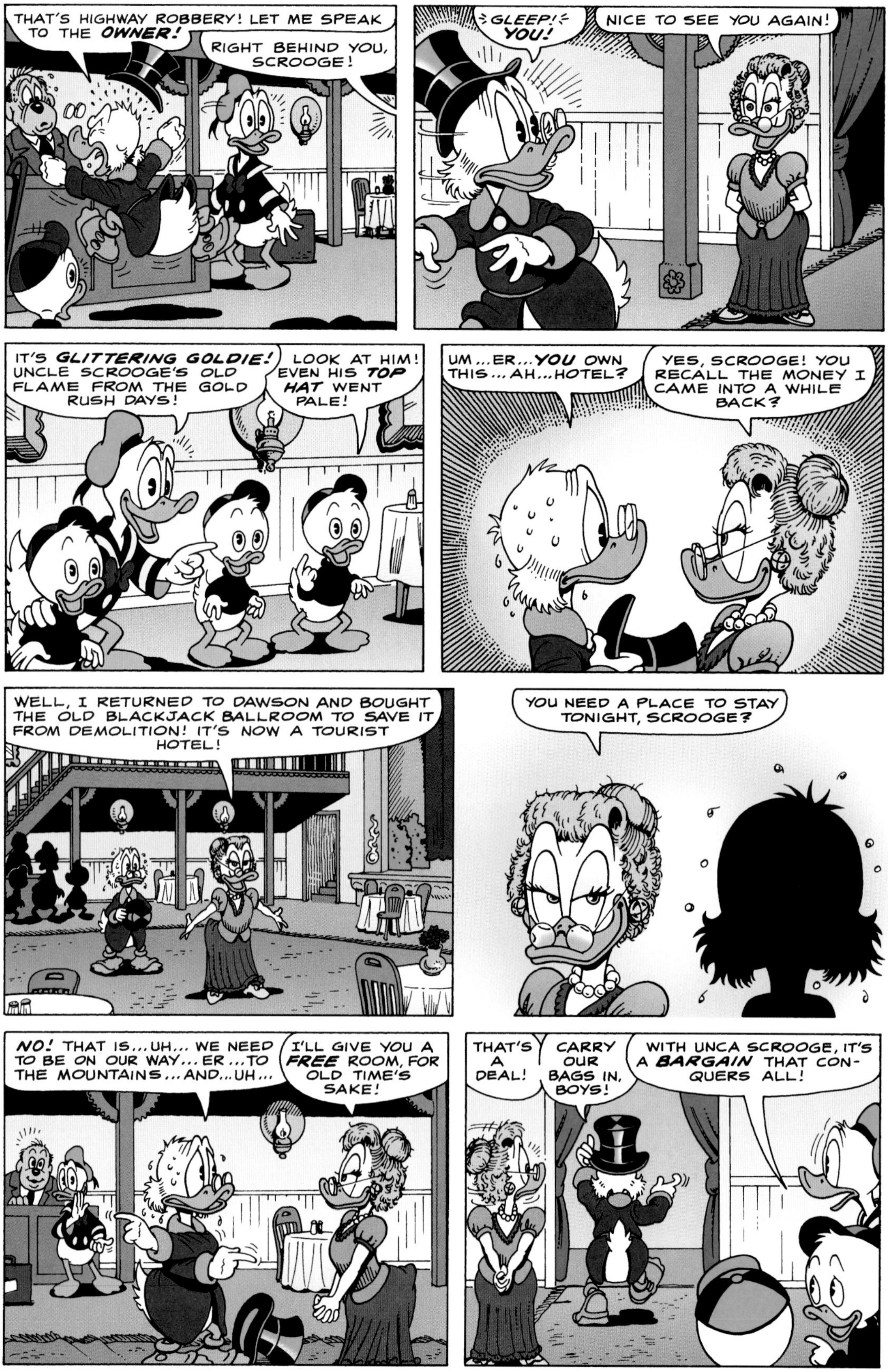

THAT'S HIGHWAY ROBBERY! LET ME SPEAK TO THE OWNER!
RIGHT BEHIND YOU, SCROOGE!
GLEEP! YOU!
NICE TO SEE YOU AGAIN!
IT'S GLITTERING GOLDIE! UNCLE SCROOGE'S OLD FLAME FROM THE GOLD RUSH DAYS!
LOOK AT HIM! EVEN HIS TOP HAT WENT PALE!
UM... ER... YOU OWN THIS... AH... HOTEL?
YES, SCROOGE! YOU RECALL THE MONEY I CAME INTO A WHILE BACK?
WELL, I RETURNED TO DAWSON AND BOUGHT THE OLD BLACKJACK BALLROOM TO SAVE IT FROM DEMOLITION! IT'S NOW A TOURIST HOTEL!
YOU NEED A PLACE TO STAY TONIGHT, SCROOGE?
NO! THAT IS... UH... WE NEED TO BE ON OUR WAY... ER... TO THE MOUNTAINS... AND... UH...
I'LL GIVE YOU A FREE ROOM, FOR OLD TIME'S SAKE!
THAT'S A DEAL!
CARRY OUR BAGS IN, BOYS!
WITH UNCA SCROOGE, IT'S A BARGAIN THAT CONQUERS ALL!

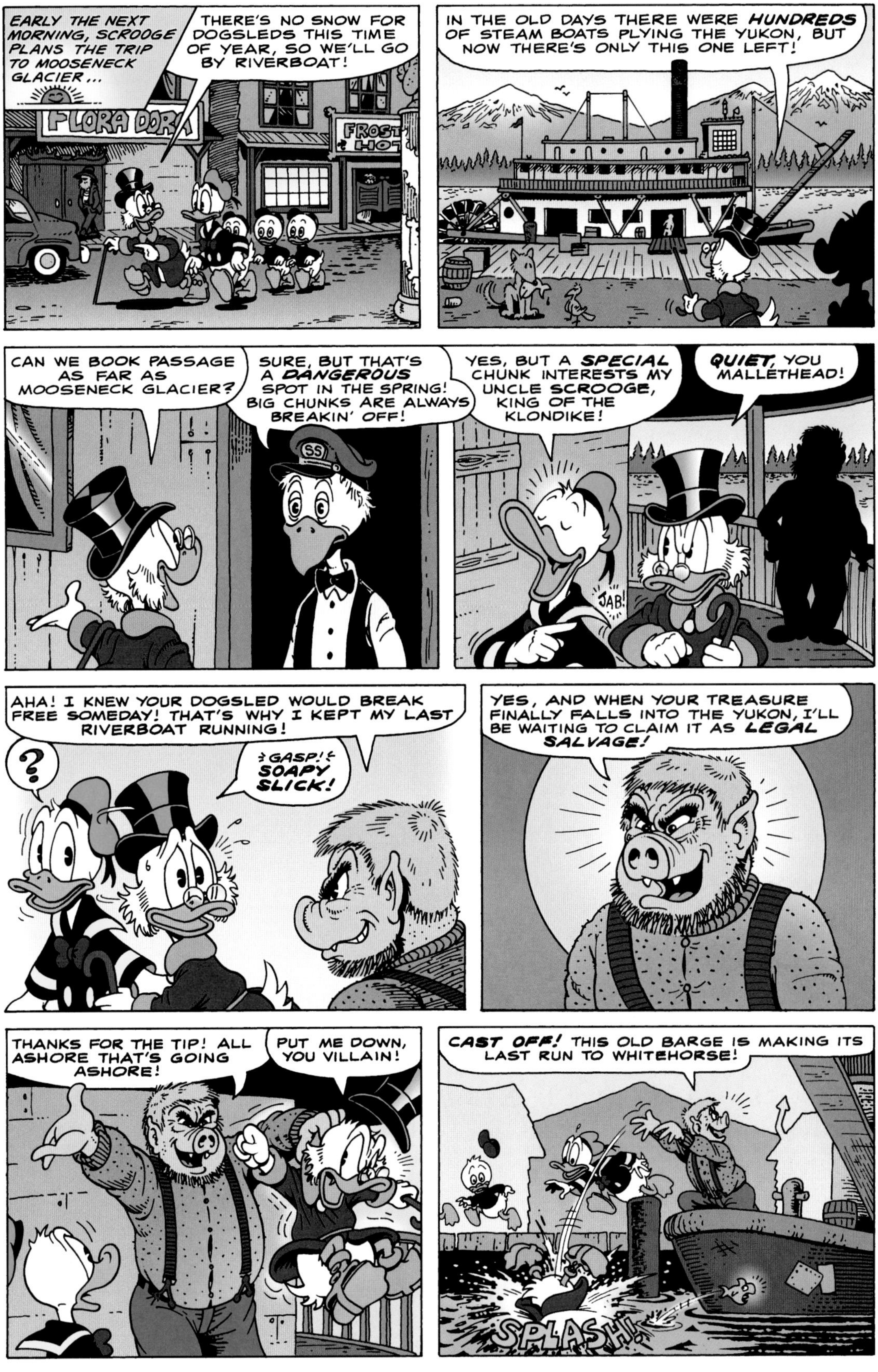
EARLY THE NEXT MORNING, SCROOGE PLANS THE TRIP TO MOOSENECK GLACIER...
THERE'S NO SNOW FOR DOGSLEDS THIS TIME OF YEAR, SO WE'LL GO BY RIVERBOAT!
FLORA DOR
FROST HOT
IN THE OLD DAYS THERE WERE HUNDREDS OF STEAM BOATS PLYING THE YUKON, BUT NOW THERE'S ONLY THIS ONE LEFT!
CAN WE BOOK PASSAGE AS FAR AS MOOSENECK GLACIER?
SURE, BUT THAT'S A DANGEROUS SPOT IN THE SPRING! BIG CHUNKS ARE ALWAYS BREAKIN' OFF!
SS
YES, BUT A SPECIAL CHUNK INTERESTS MY UNCLE SCROOGE, KING OF THE KLONDIKE!
QUIET, YOU MALLETHEAD!
JAB!
AHA! I KNEW YOUR DOGSLED WOULD BREAK FREE SOMEDAY! THAT'S WHY I KEPT MY LAST RIVERBOAT RUNNING!
?
GASP! SOAPY SLICK!
YES, AND WHEN YOUR TREASURE FINALLY FALLS INTO THE YUKON, I'LL BE WAITING TO CLAIM IT AS LEGAL SALVAGE!
THANKS FOR THE TIP! ALL ASHORE THAT'S GOING ASHORE!
PUT ME DOWN, YOU VILLAIN!
CAST OFF! THIS OLD BARGE IS MAKING ITS LAST RUN TO WHITEHORSE!
SPLASH!

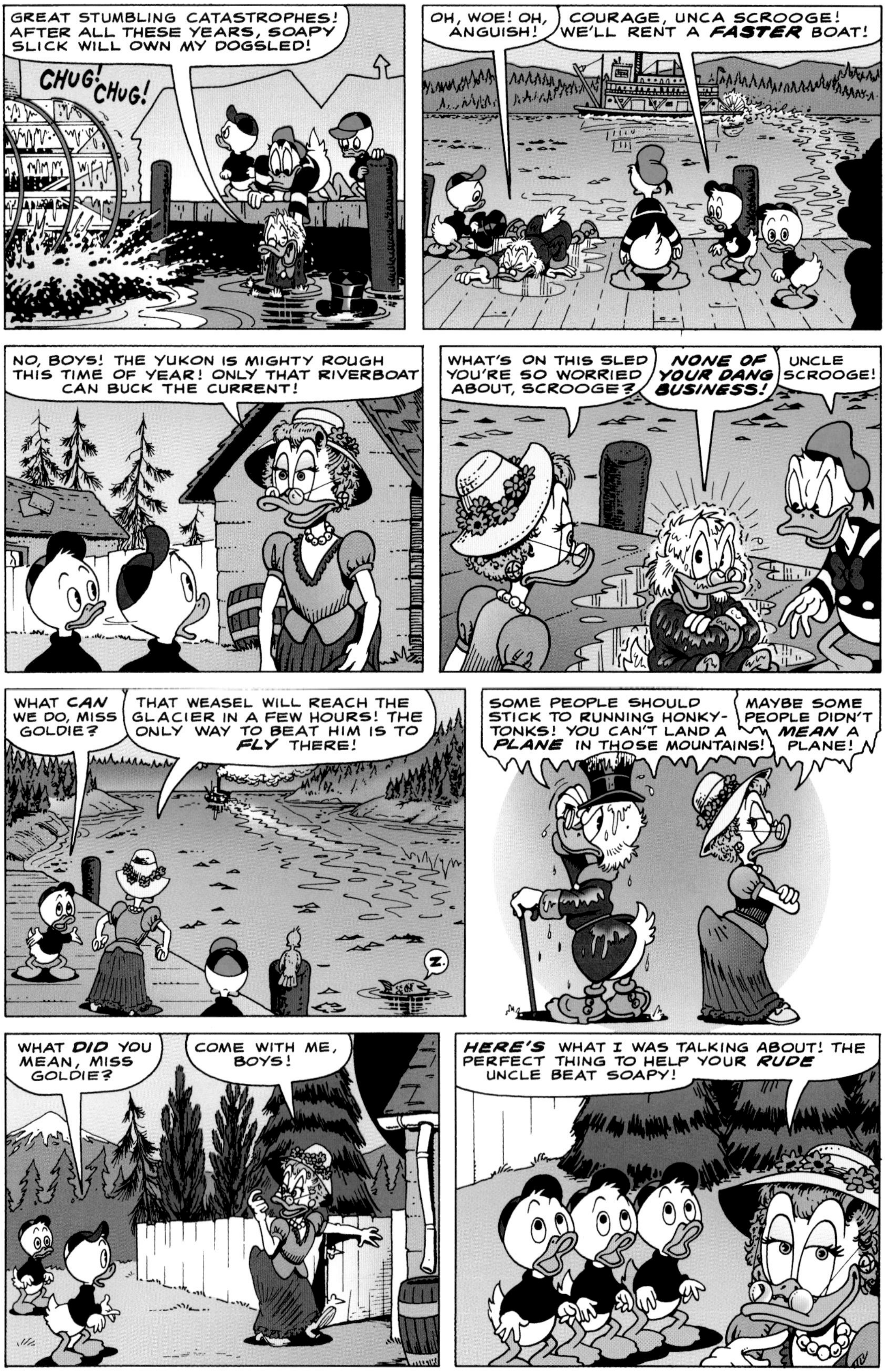
GREAT STUMBLING CATASTROPHES! AFTER ALL THESE YEARS, SOAPY SLICK WILL OWN MY DOGSLED!
CHUG! CHUG!
OH, WOE! OH, ANGUISH!
COURAGE, UNCA SCROOGE! WE'LL RENT A FASTER BOAT!
NO, BOYS! THE YUKON IS MIGHTY ROUGH THIS TIME OF YEAR! ONLY THAT RIVERBOAT CAN BUCK THE CURRENT!
WHAT'S ON THIS SLED YOU'RE SO WORRIED ABOUT, SCROOGE?
NONE OF YOUR DANG BUSINESS!
UNCLE SCROOGE!
WHAT CAN WE DO, MISS GOLDIE?
THAT WEASEL WILL REACH THE GLACIER IN A FEW HOURS! THE ONLY WAY TO BEAT HIM IS TO FLY THERE!
Z.
SOME PEOPLE SHOULD STICK TO RUNNING HONKY-TONKS! YOU CAN'T LAND A PLANE IN THOSE MOUNTAINS!
MAYBE SOME PEOPLE DIDN'T MEAN A PLANE!
WHAT DID YOU MEAN, MISS GOLDIE?
COME WITH ME, BOYS!
HERE'S WHAT I WAS TALKING ABOUT! THE PERFECT THING TO HELP YOUR RUDE UNCLE BEAT SOAPY!

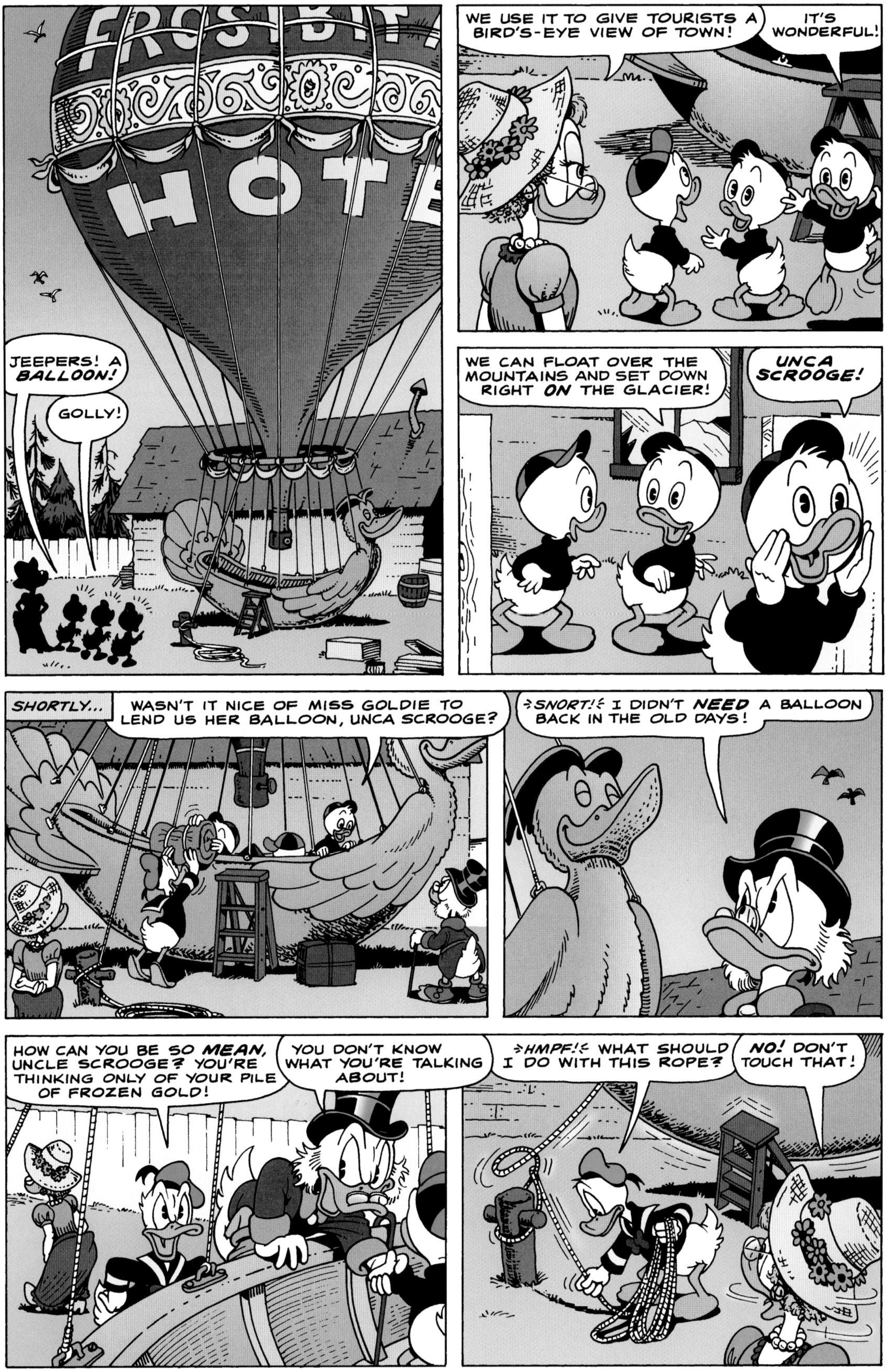
JEEPERS! A BALLOON!
GOLLY!
FROSTBITE
HOTE
WE USE IT TO GIVE TOURISTS A BIRD'S-EYE VIEW OF TOWN!
IT'S WONDERFUL!
WE CAN FLOAT OVER THE MOUNTAINS AND SET DOWN RIGHT ON THE GLACIER!
UNCA SCROOGE!
SHORTLY...
WASN'T IT NICE OF MISS GOLDIE TO LEND US HER BALLOON, UNCA SCROOGE?
SNORT! I DIDN'T NEED A BALLOON BACK IN THE OLD DAYS!
HOW CAN YOU BE SO MEAN, UNCLE SCROOGE? YOU'RE THINKING ONLY OF YOUR PILE OF FROZEN GOLD!
YOU DON'T KNOW WHAT YOU'RE TALKING ABOUT!
HMPF! WHAT SHOULD I DO WITH THIS ROPE?
NO! DON'T TOUCH THAT!

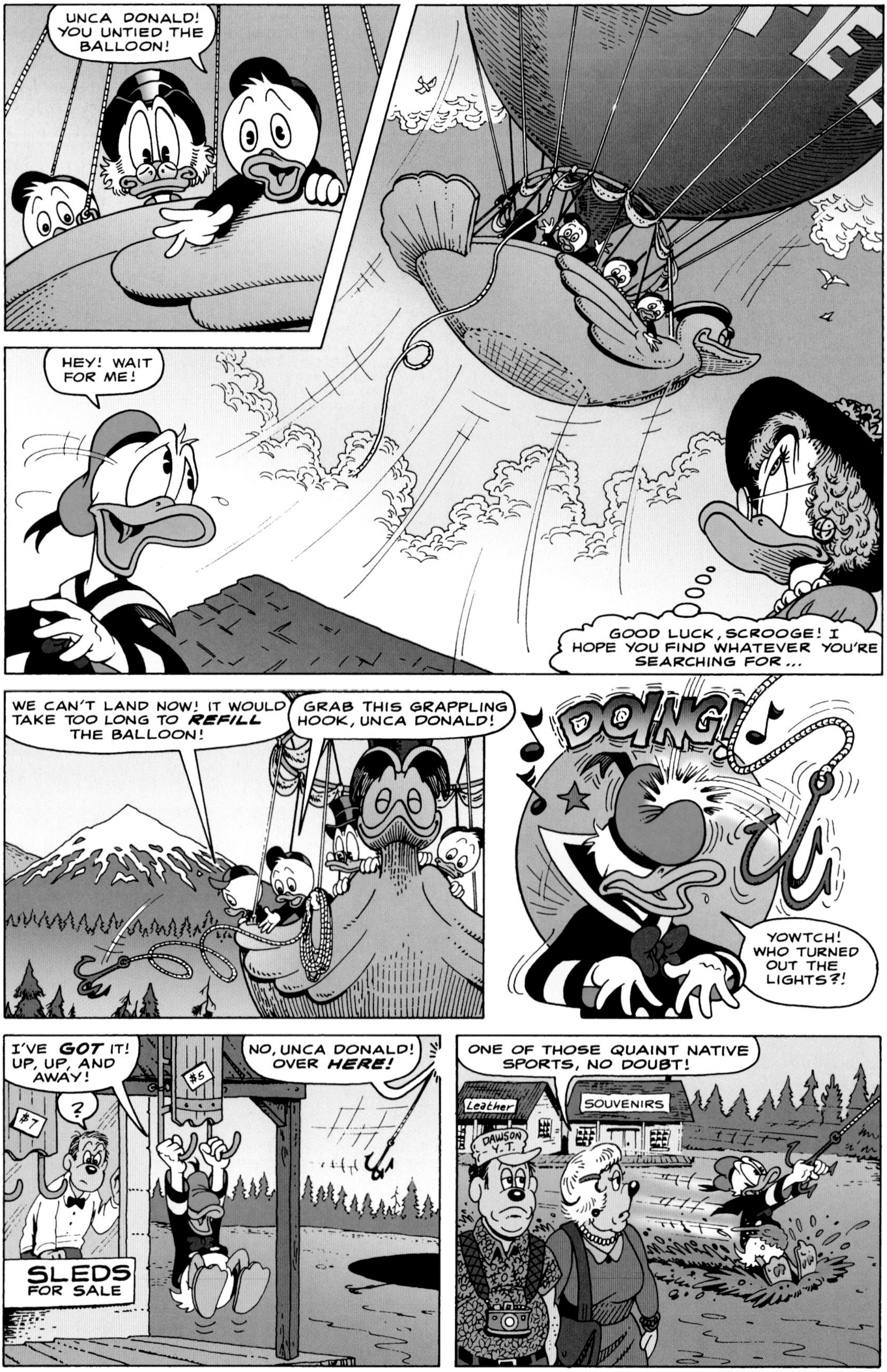
UNCA DONALD! YOU UNTIED THE BALLOON!
HEY! WAIT FOR ME!
GOOD LUCK, SCROOGE! I HOPE YOU FIND WHATEVER YOU'RE SEARCHING FOR...
WE CAN'T LAND NOW! IT WOULD TAKE TOO LONG TO REFILL THE BALLOON!
GRAB THIS GRAPPLING HOOK, UNCA DONALD!
DOING!
YOWTCH! WHO TURNED OUT THE LIGHTS?!
I'VE GOT IT! UP, UP, AND AWAY!
NO, UNCA DONALD! OVER HERE!
#7
?
#5
SLEDS FOR SALE
ONE OF THOSE QUAINT NATIVE SPORTS, NO DOUBT!
Leather
SOUVENIRS
DAWSON Y.T.

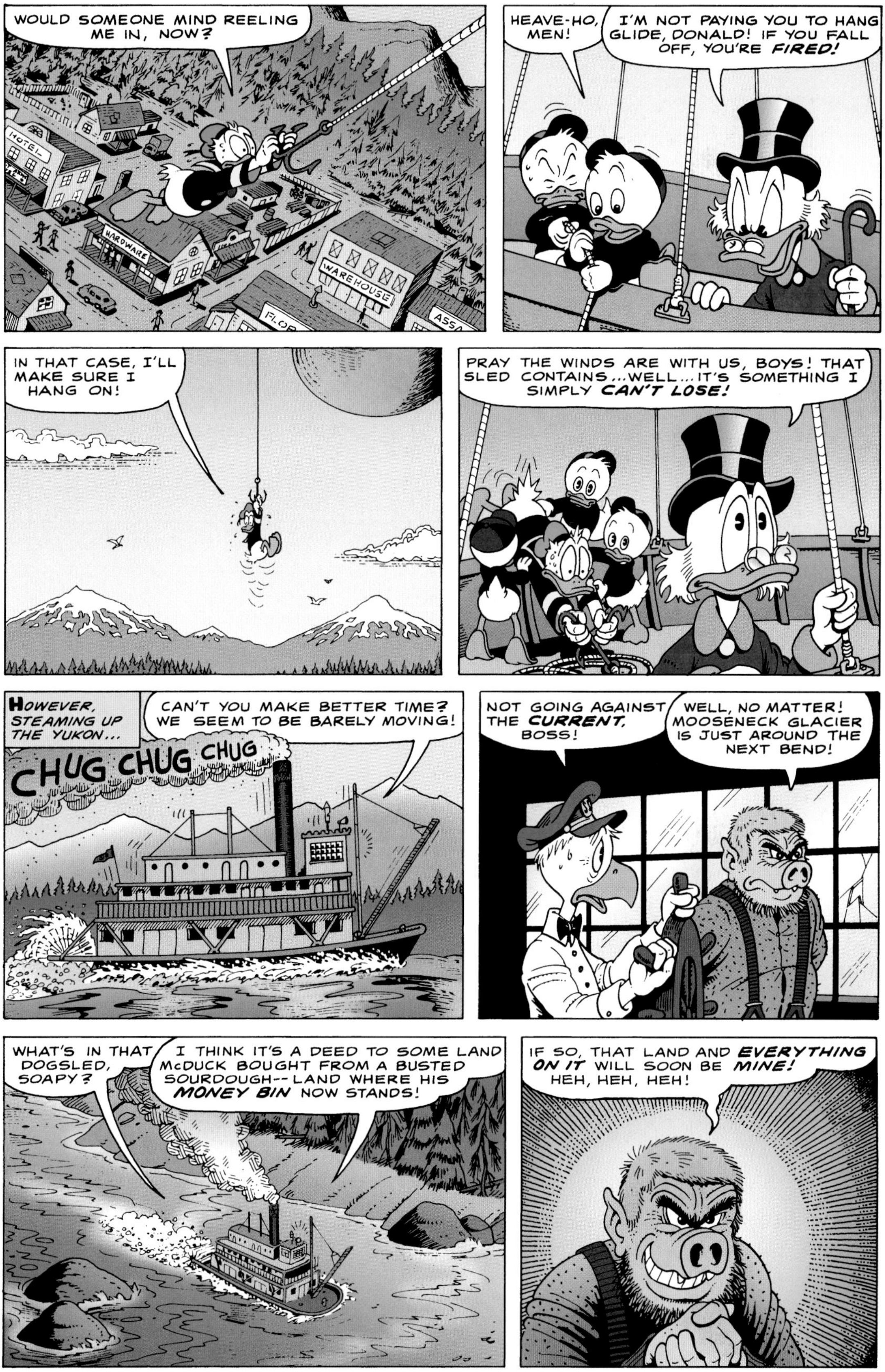
WOULD SOMEONE MIND REELING ME IN, NOW?
HOTEL
HARDWARE
WAREHOUSE
HEAVE-HO, MEN!
I'M NOT PAYING YOU TO HANG GLIDE, DONALD! IF YOU FALL OFF, YOU'RE FIRED!
IN THAT CASE, I'LL MAKE SURE I HANG ON!
PRAY THE WINDS ARE WITH US, BOYS! THAT SLED CONTAINS...WELL...IT'S SOMETHING I SIMPLY CAN'T LOSE!
HOWEVER, STEAMING UP THE YUKON...
CAN'T YOU MAKE BETTER TIME? WE SEEM TO BE BARELY MOVING!
CHUG CHUG CHUG
NOT GOING AGAINST THE CURRENT, BOSS!
WELL, NO MATTER! MOOSENECK GLACIER IS JUST AROUND THE NEXT BEND!
WHAT'S IN THAT DOGSLED, SOAPY?
I THINK IT'S A DEED TO SOME LAND McDUCK BOUGHT FROM A BUSTED SOURDOUGH--LAND WHERE HIS MONEY BIN NOW STANDS!
IF SO, THAT LAND AND EVERYTHING ON IT WILL SOON BE MINE! HEH, HEH, HEH!

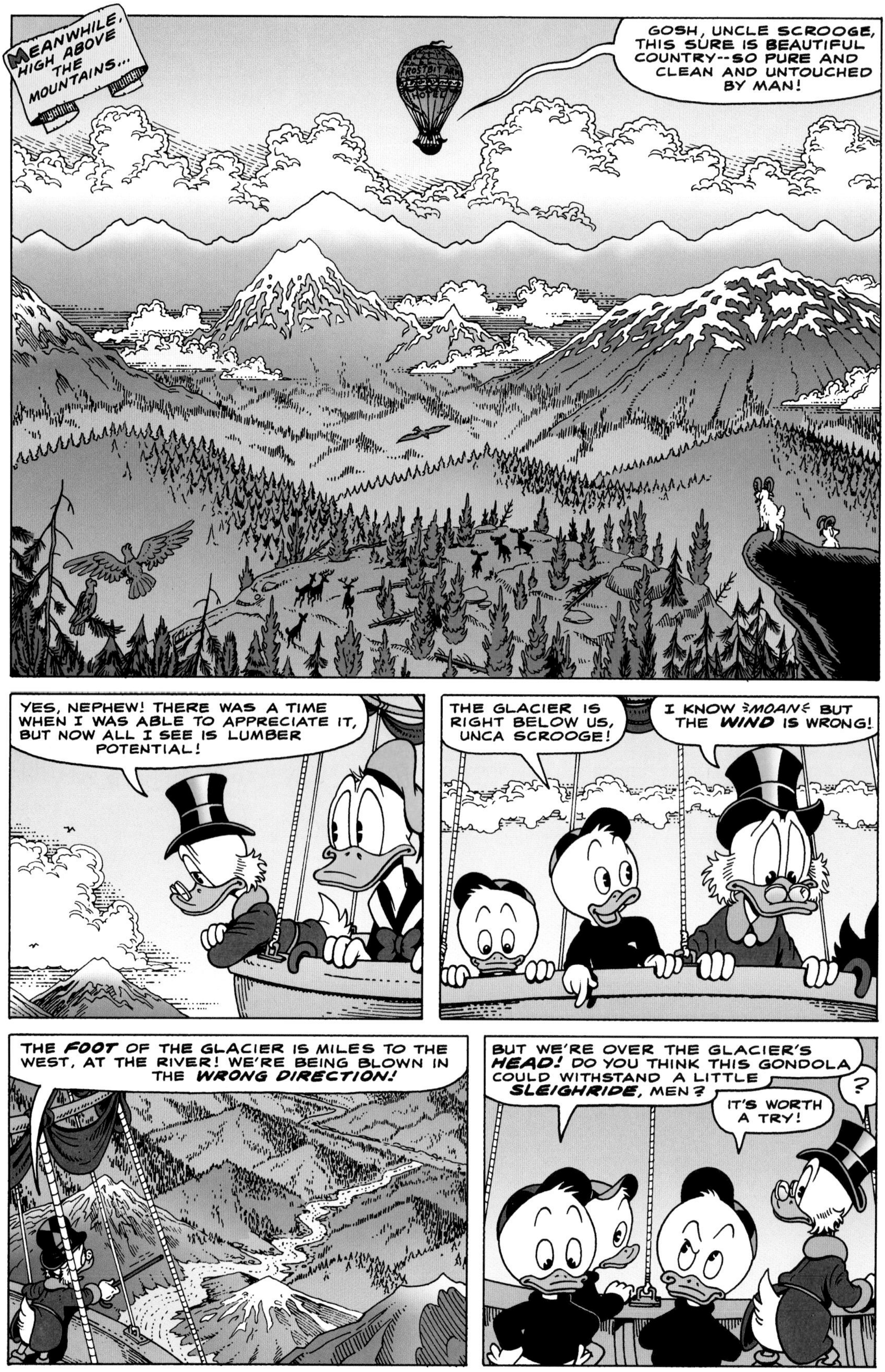

MEANWHILE, HIGH ABOVE THE MOUNTAINS...
GOSH, UNCLE SCROOGE, THIS SURE IS BEAUTIFUL COUNTRY--SO PURE AND CLEAN AND UNTOUCHED BY MAN!
YES, NEPHEW! THERE WAS A TIME WHEN I WAS ABLE TO APPRECIATE IT, BUT NOW ALL I SEE IS LUMBER POTENTIAL!
THE GLACIER IS RIGHT BELOW US, UNCA SCROOGE!
I KNOW ≷MOAN≶ BUT THE WIND IS WRONG!
THE FOOT OF THE GLACIER IS MILES TO THE WEST, AT THE RIVER! WE'RE BEING BLOWN IN THE WRONG DIRECTION!
BUT WE'RE OVER THE GLACIER'S HEAD! DO YOU THINK THIS GONDOLA COULD WITHSTAND A LITTLE SLEIGHRIDE, MEN?
?
IT'S WORTH A TRY!

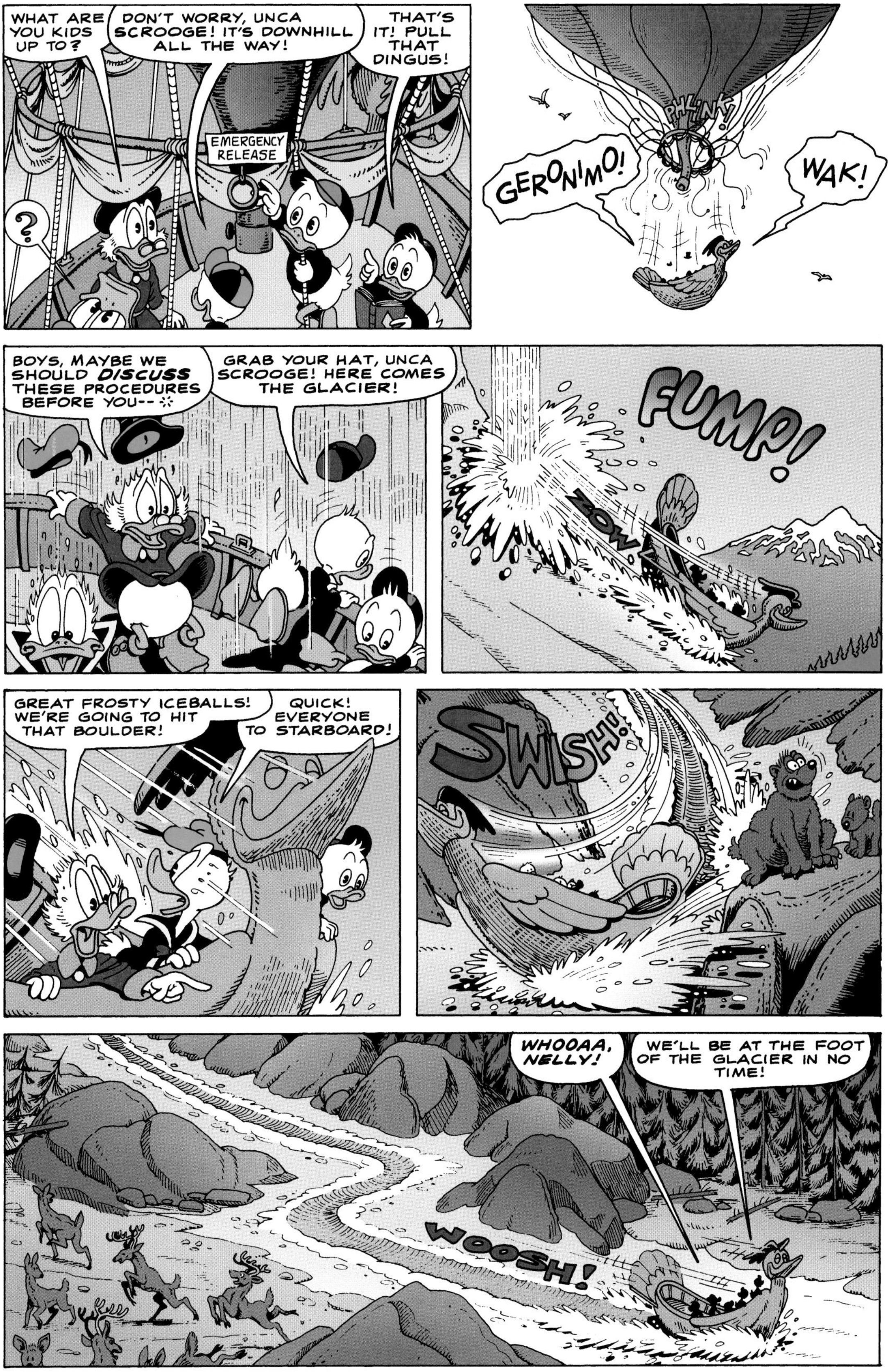
WHAT ARE YOU KIDS UP TO?
DON'T WORRY, UNCA SCROOGE! IT'S DOWNHILL ALL THE WAY!
THAT'S IT! PULL THAT DINGUS!
EMERGENCY RELEASE
?
PHLINK!
GERONIMO!
WAK!
BOYS, MAYBE WE SHOULD DISCUSS THESE PROCEDURES BEFORE YOU--
GRAB YOUR HAT, UNCA SCROOGE! HERE COMES THE GLACIER!
FUMP!
ZOW
GREAT FROSTY ICEBALLS! WE'RE GOING TO HIT THAT BOULDER!
QUICK! EVERYONE TO STARBOARD!
SWISH!
WHOOAA, NELLY!
WE'LL BE AT THE FOOT OF THE GLACIER IN NO TIME!
WOOSH!

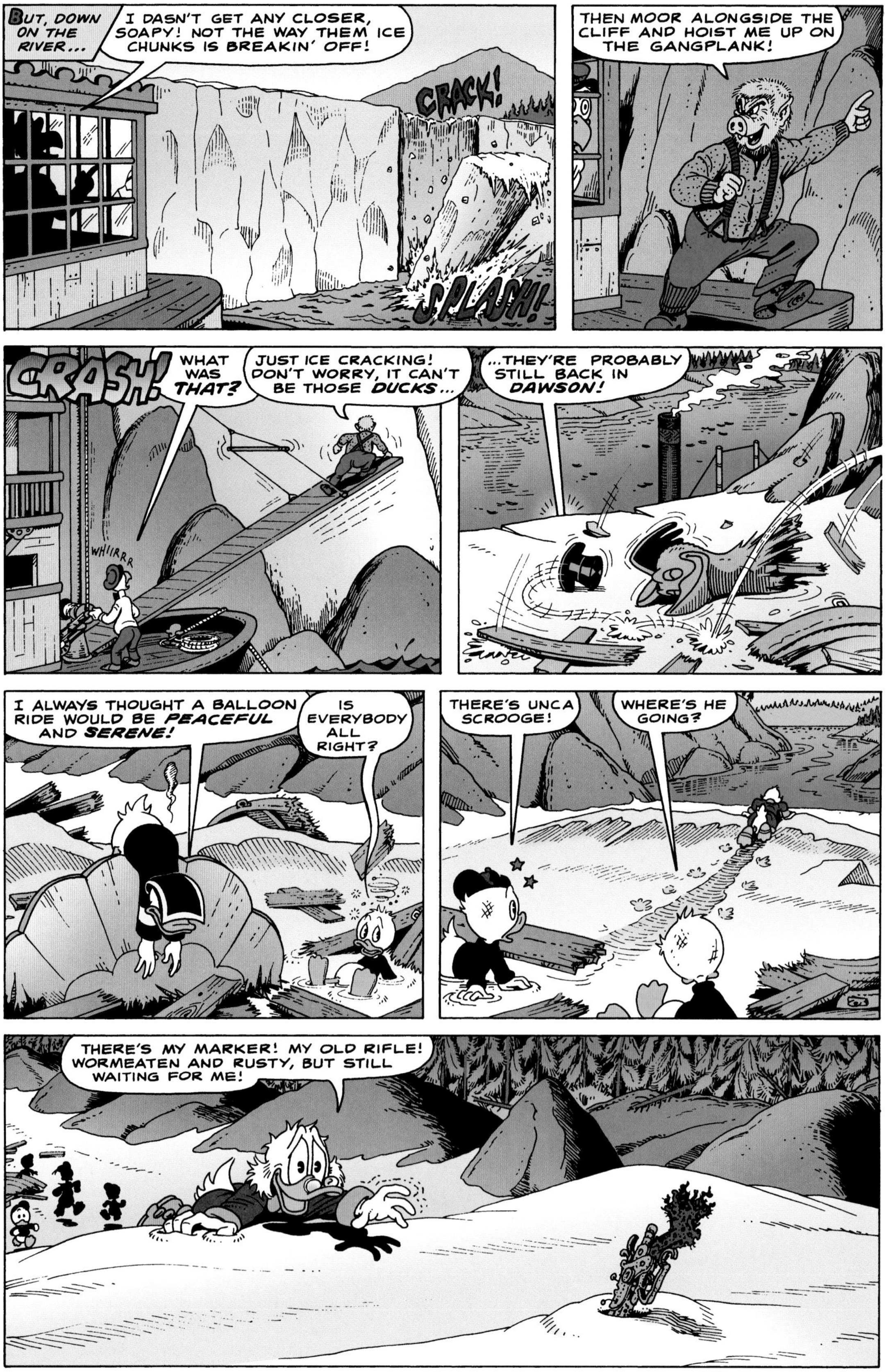
BUT, DOWN ON THE RIVER...
I DASN'T GET ANY CLOSER, SOAPY! NOT THE WAY THEM ICE CHUNKS IS BREAKIN' OFF!
CRACK!
SPLASH!
THEN MOOR ALONGSIDE THE CLIFF AND HOIST ME UP ON THE GANGPLANK!
CRASH!
WHAT WAS THAT?
JUST ICE CRACKING! DON'T WORRY, IT CAN'T BE THOSE DUCKS...
WHIRRR
...THEY'RE PROBABLY STILL BACK IN DAWSON!
I ALWAYS THOUGHT A BALLOON RIDE WOULD BE PEACEFUL AND SERENE!
IS EVERYBODY ALL RIGHT?
THERE'S UNCA SCROOGE!
WHERE'S HE GOING?
THERE'S MY MARKER! MY OLD RIFLE! WORMEATEN AND RUSTY, BUT STILL WAITING FOR ME!

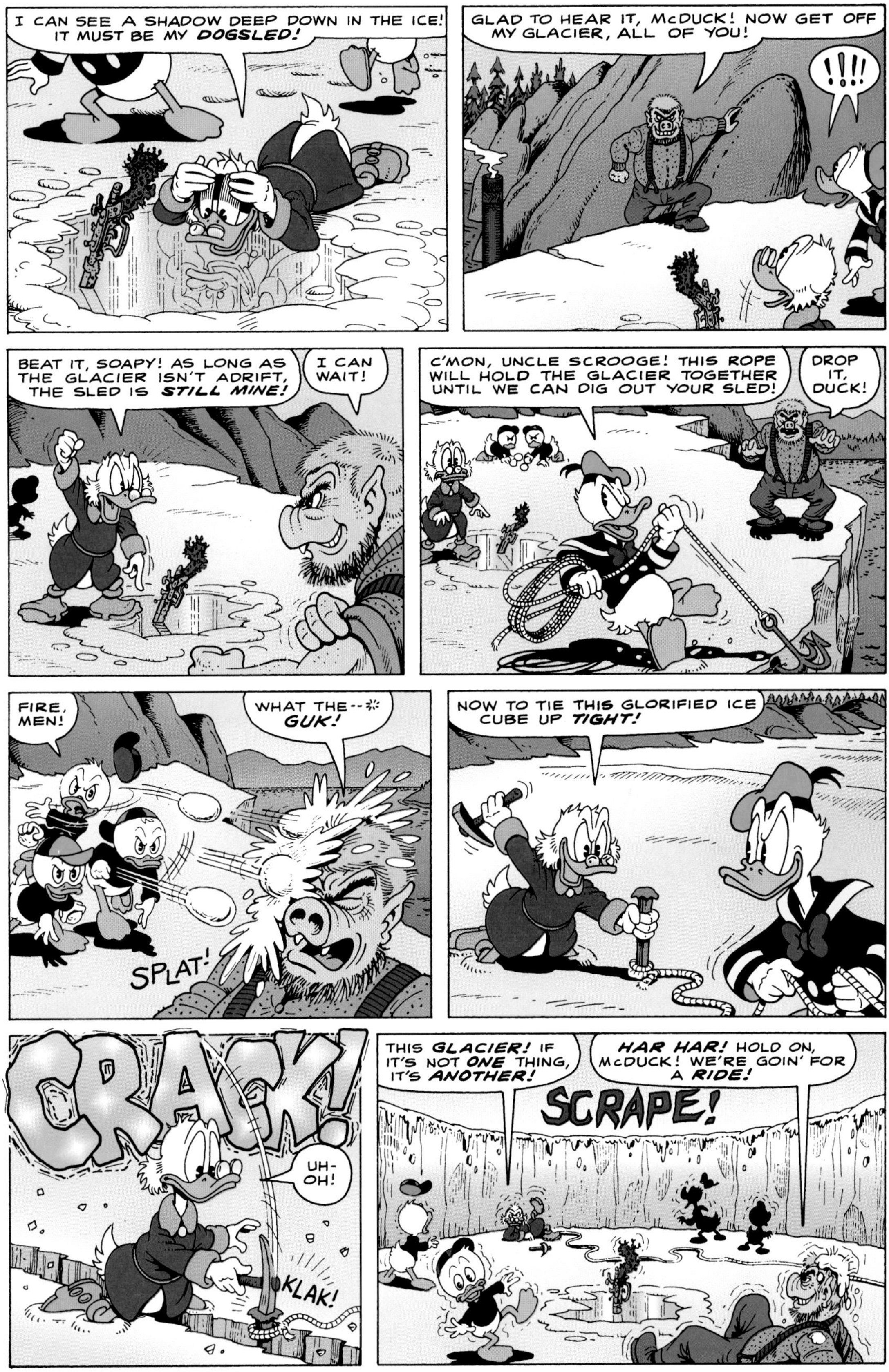
I CAN SEE A SHADOW DEEP DOWN IN THE ICE! IT MUST BE MY DOGSLED!
GLAD TO HEAR IT, McDUCK! NOW GET OFF MY GLACIER, ALL OF YOU!
!!!!
BEAT IT, SOAPY! AS LONG AS THE GLACIER ISN'T ADRIFT, THE SLED IS STILL MINE!
I CAN WAIT!
C'MON, UNCLE SCROOGE! THIS ROPE WILL HOLD THE GLACIER TOGETHER UNTIL WE CAN DIG OUT YOUR SLED!
DROP IT, DUCK!
FIRE, MEN!
WHAT THE--
GUK!
SPLAT!
NOW TO TIE THIS GLORIFIED ICE CUBE UP TIGHT!
CRACK!
UH-OH!
KLAK!
THIS GLACIER! IF IT'S NOT ONE THING, IT'S ANOTHER!
HAR HAR! HOLD ON, McDUCK! WE'RE GOIN' FOR A RIDE!
SCRAPE!

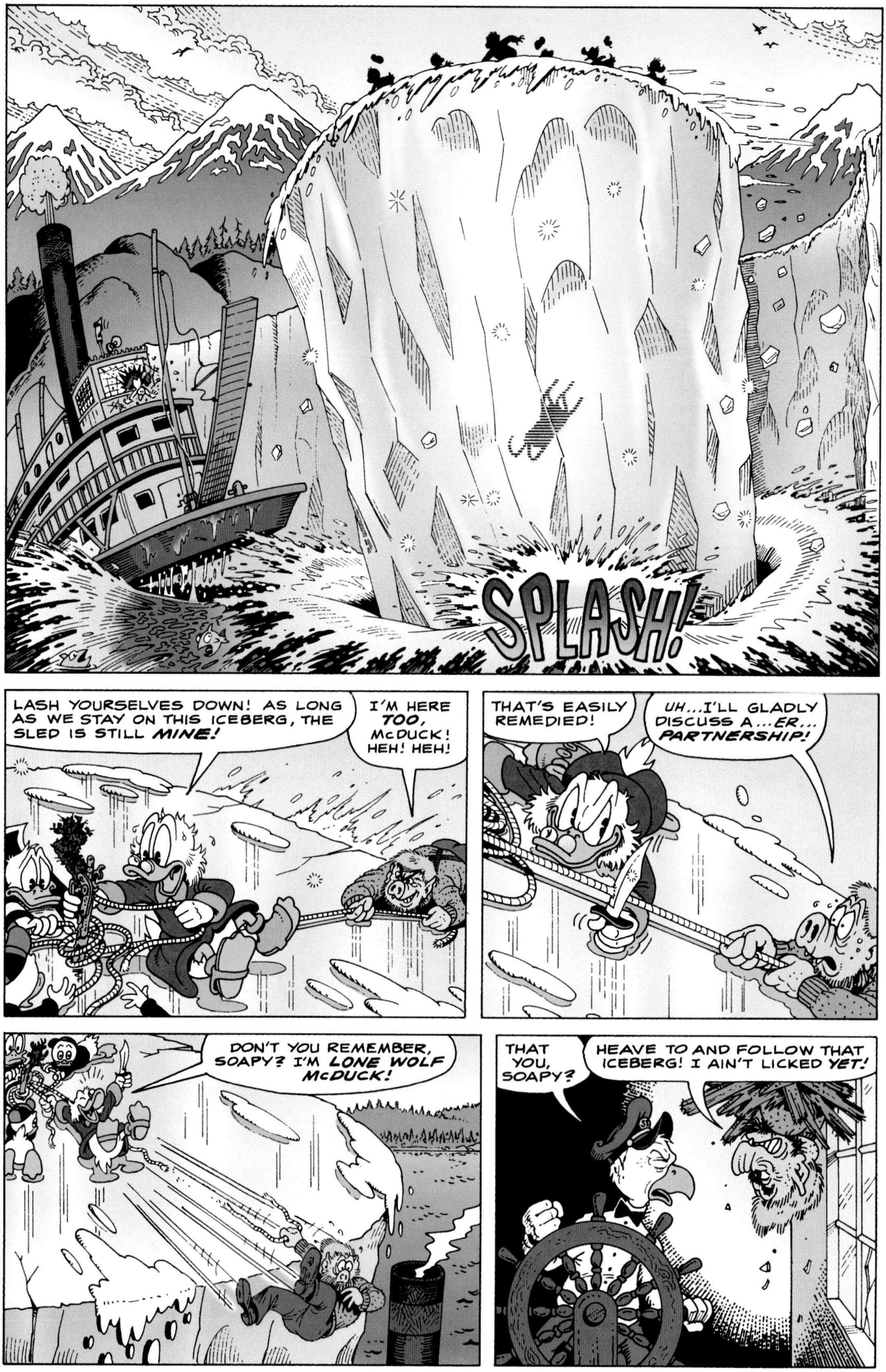
SPLASH!
LASH YOURSELVES DOWN! AS LONG AS WE STAY ON THIS ICEBERG, THE SLED IS STILL MINE!
I'M HERE TOO, McDUCK! HEH! HEH!
THAT'S EASILY REMEDIED!
UH...I'LL GLADLY DISCUSS A...ER... PARTNERSHIP!
DON'T YOU REMEMBER, SOAPY? I'M LONE WOLF McDUCK!
THAT YOU, SOAPY?
HEAVE TO AND FOLLOW THAT ICEBERG! I AIN'T LICKED YET!

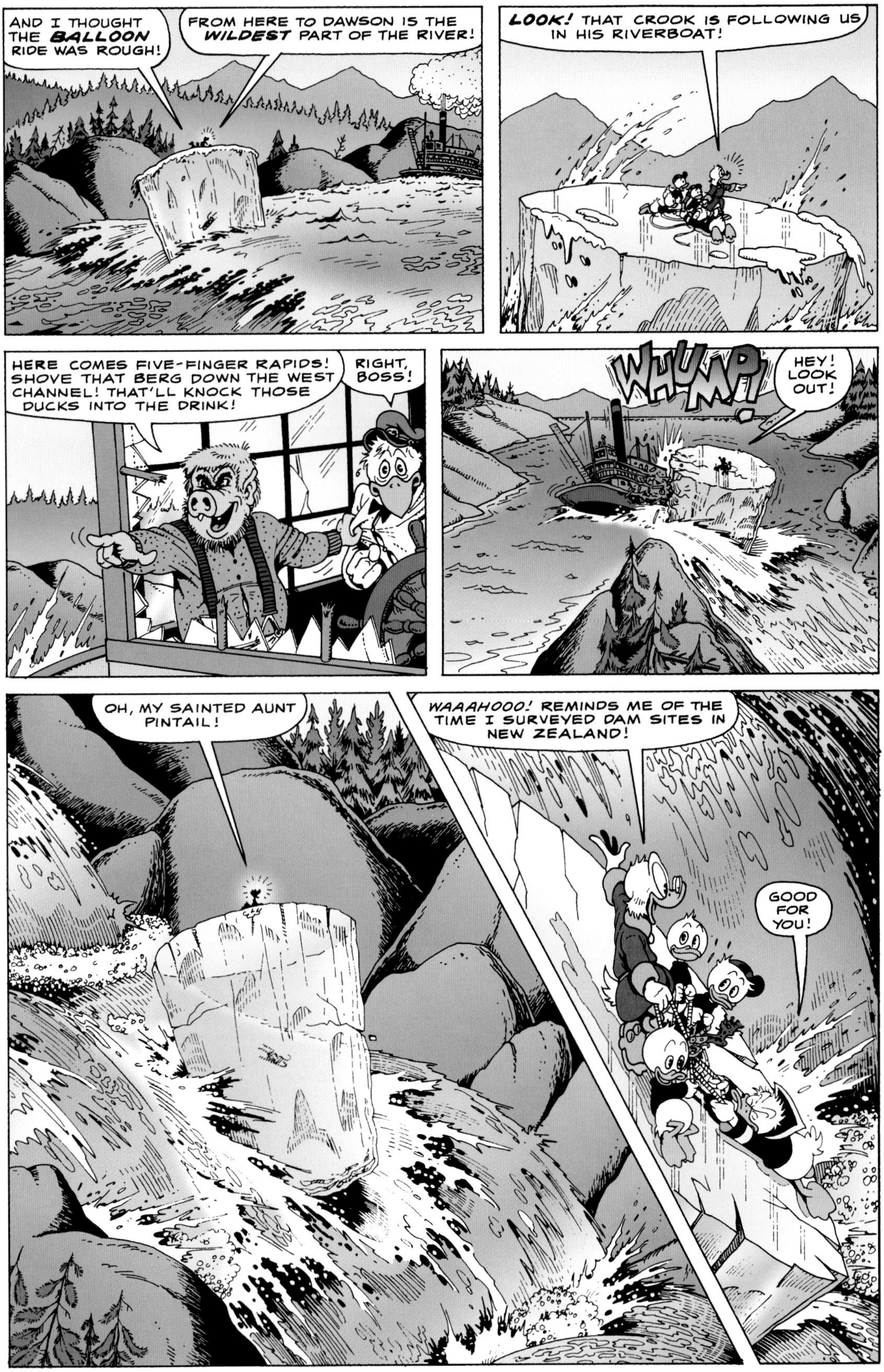
AND I THOUGHT THE BALLOON RIDE WAS ROUGH!
FROM HERE TO DAWSON IS THE WILDEST PART OF THE RIVER!
LOOK! THAT CROOK IS FOLLOWING US IN HIS RIVERBOAT!
HERE COMES FIVE-FINGER RAPIDS! SHOVE THAT BERG DOWN THE WEST CHANNEL! THAT'LL KNOCK THOSE DUCKS INTO THE DRINK!
RIGHT, BOSS!
WHUMP!
HEY! LOOK OUT!
OH, MY SAINTED AUNT PINTAIL!
WAAAHOOO! REMINDS ME OF THE TIME I SURVEYED DAM SITES IN NEW ZEALAND!
GOOD FOR YOU!

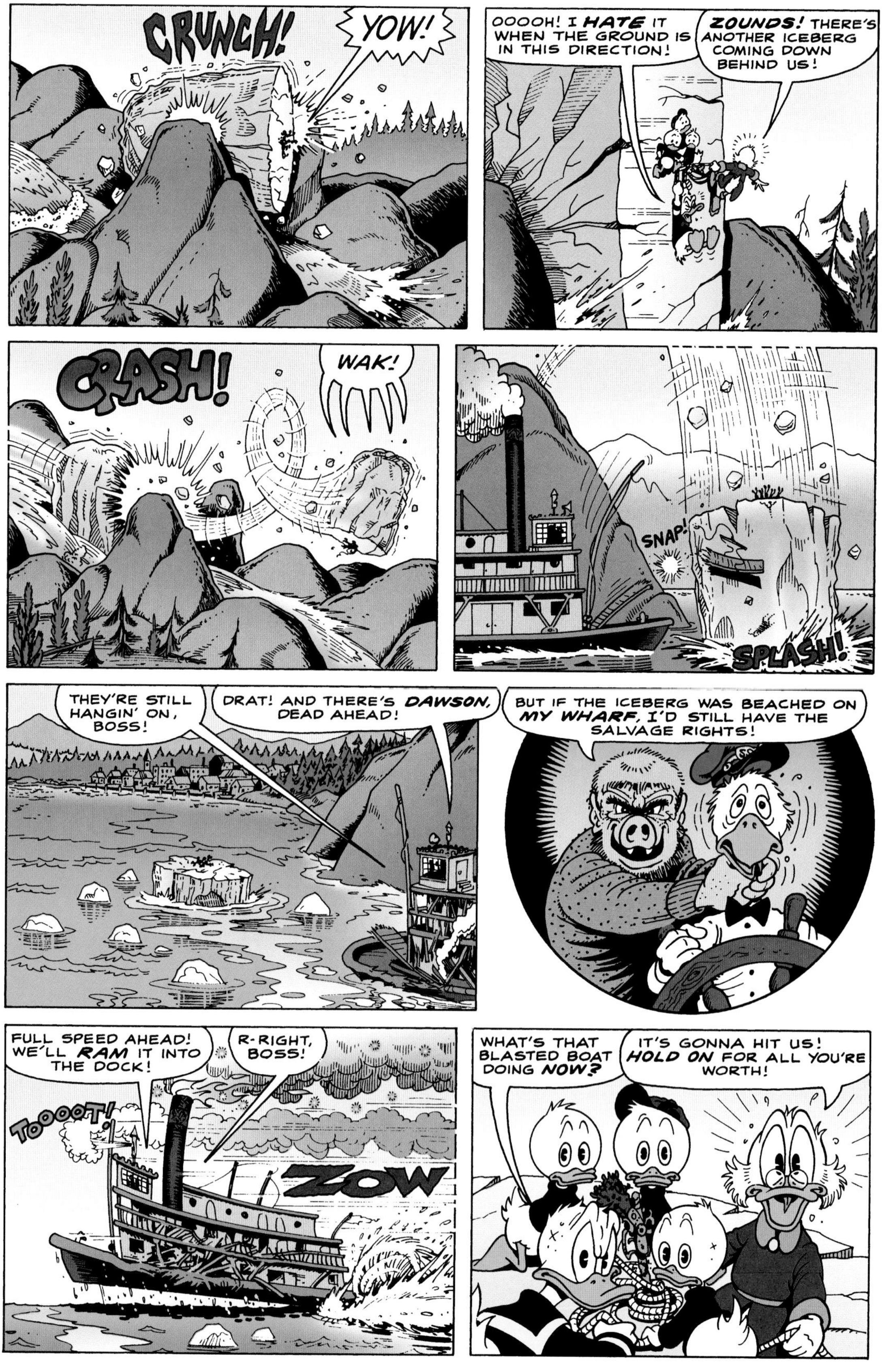
CRUNCH!
YOW!
OOOOH! I HATE IT WHEN THE GROUND IS IN THIS DIRECTION!
ZOUNDS! THERE'S ANOTHER ICEBERG COMING DOWN BEHIND US!
CRASH!
WAK!
SNAP!
SPLASH!
THEY'RE STILL HANGIN' ON, BOSS!
DRAT! AND THERE'S DAWSON, DEAD AHEAD!
BUT IF THE ICEBERG WAS BEACHED ON MY WHARF, I'D STILL HAVE THE SALVAGE RIGHTS!
FULL SPEED AHEAD! WE'LL RAM IT INTO THE DOCK!
R-RIGHT, BOSS!
TOOOOT!
ZOW
WHAT'S THAT BLASTED BOAT DOING NOW?
IT'S GONNA HIT US! HOLD ON FOR ALL YOU'RE WORTH!

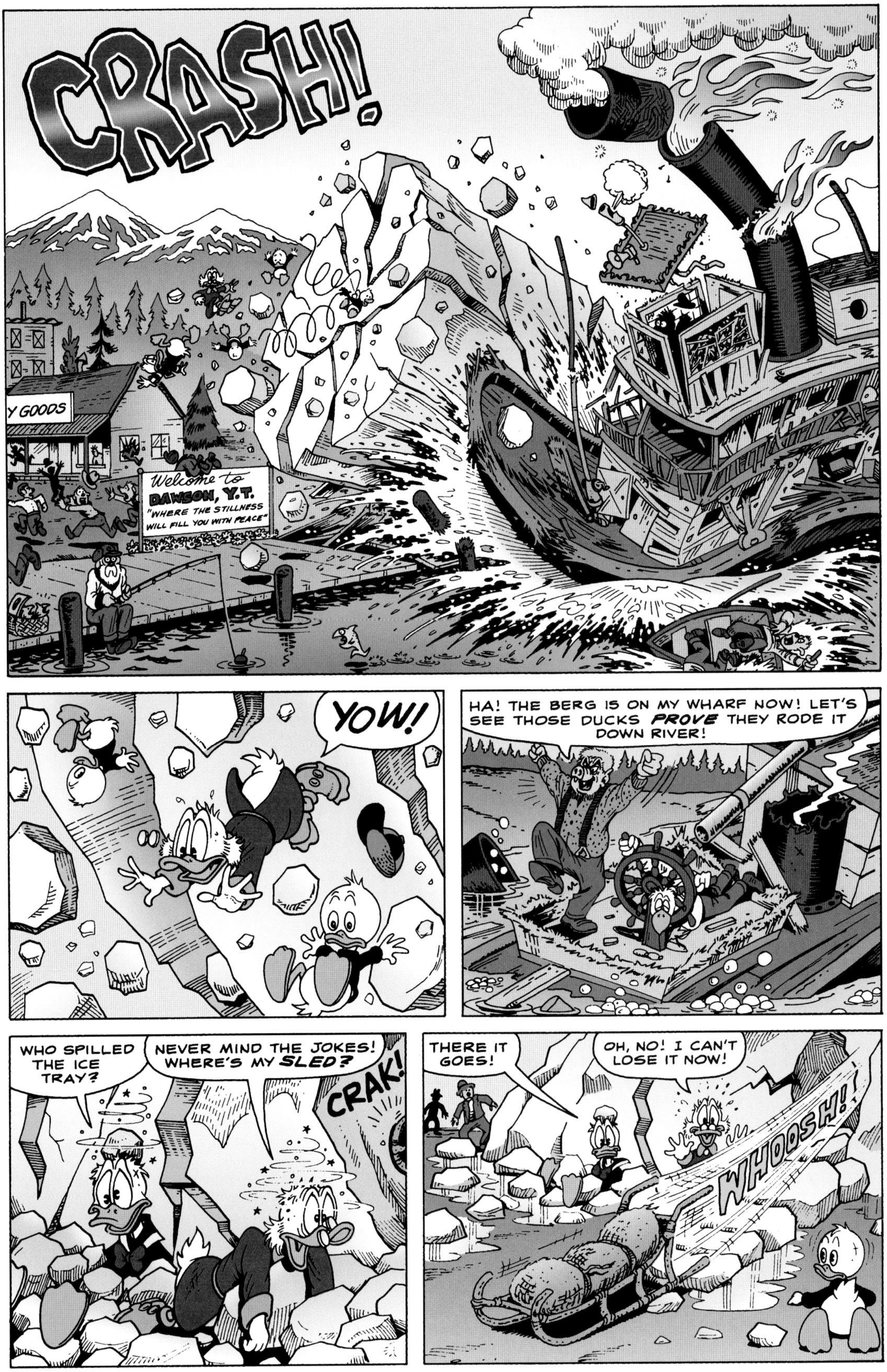
CRASH!
Y GOODS
Welcome to DAWSON, Y.T. "WHERE THE STILLNESS WILL FILL YOU WITH PEACE"
YOW!
HA! THE BERG IS ON MY WHARF NOW! LET'S SEE THOSE DUCKS PROVE THEY RODE IT DOWN RIVER!
WHO SPILLED THE ICE TRAY?
NEVER MIND THE JOKES! WHERE'S MY SLED?
CRAK!
THERE IT GOES!
OH, NO! I CAN'T LOSE IT NOW!
WHOOSH!

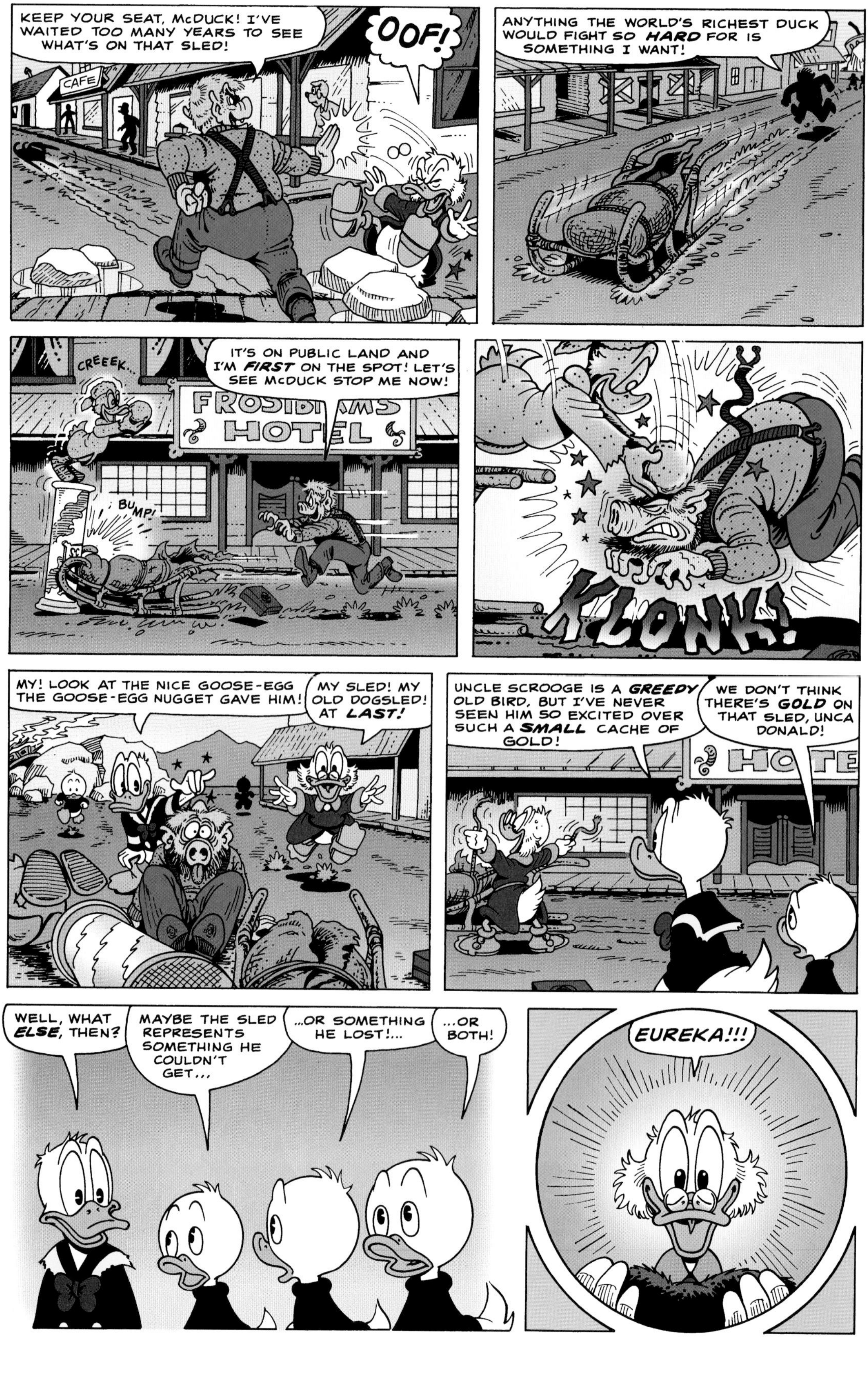
KEEP YOUR SEAT, McDUCK! I'VE WAITED TOO MANY YEARS TO SEE WHAT'S ON THAT SLED!
OOF!
CAFE
ANYTHING THE WORLD'S RICHEST DUCK WOULD FIGHT SO HARD FOR IS SOMETHING I WANT!
CREEEK...
IT'S ON PUBLIC LAND AND I'M FIRST ON THE SPOT! LET'S SEE McDUCK STOP ME NOW!
HOTEL
BUMP!
KLONK!
MY! LOOK AT THE NICE GOOSE-EGG THE GOOSE-EGG NUGGET GAVE HIM!
MY SLED! MY OLD DOGSLED! AT LAST!
UNCLE SCROOGE IS A GREEDY OLD BIRD, BUT I'VE NEVER SEEN HIM SO EXCITED OVER SUCH A SMALL CACHE OF GOLD!
WE DON'T THINK THERE'S GOLD ON THAT SLED, UNCA DONALD!
WELL, WHAT ELSE, THEN?
MAYBE THE SLED REPRESENTS SOMETHING HE COULDN'T GET...
...OR SOMETHING HE LOST!...
...OR BOTH!
EUREKA!!!

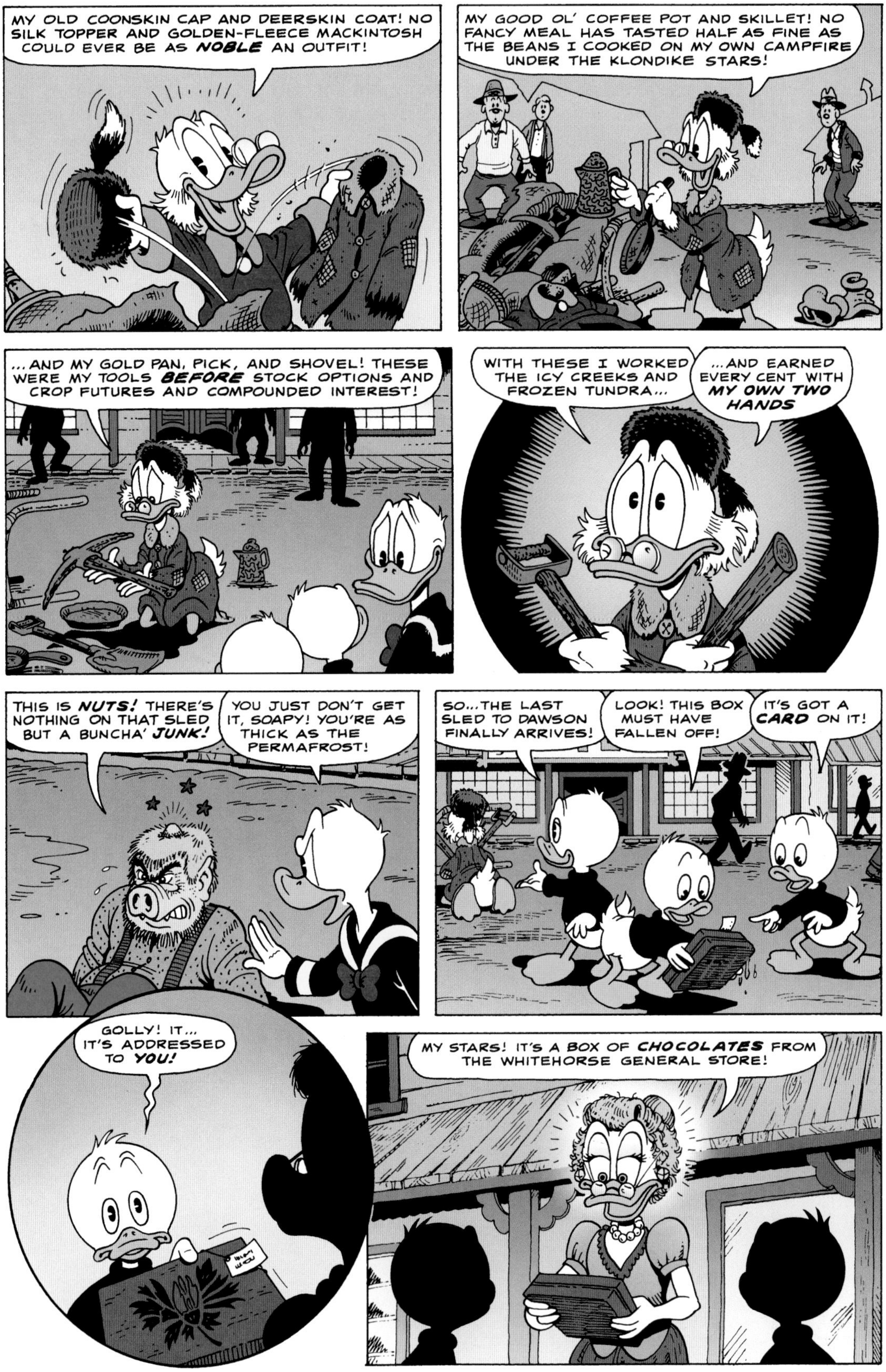
MY OLD COONSKIN CAP AND DEERSKIN COAT! NO SILK TOPPER AND GOLDEN-FLEECE MACKINTOSH COULD EVER BE AS NOBLE AN OUTFIT!
MY GOOD OL' COFFEE POT AND SKILLET! NO FANCY MEAL HAS TASTED HALF AS FINE AS THE BEANS I COOKED ON MY OWN CAMPFIRE UNDER THE KLONDIKE STARS!
...AND MY GOLD PAN, PICK, AND SHOVEL! THESE WERE MY TOOLS BEFORE STOCK OPTIONS AND CROP FUTURES AND COMPOUNDED INTEREST!
WITH THESE I WORKED THE ICY CREEKS AND FROZEN TUNDRA...
...AND EARNED EVERY CENT WITH MY OWN TWO HANDS
THIS IS NUTS! THERE'S NOTHING ON THAT SLED BUT A BUNCHA' JUNK!
YOU JUST DON'T GET IT, SOAPY! YOU'RE AS THICK AS THE PERMAFROST!
SO...THE LAST SLED TO DAWSON FINALLY ARRIVES!
LOOK! THIS BOX MUST HAVE FALLEN OFF!
IT'S GOT A CARD ON IT!
GOLLY! IT... IT'S ADDRESSED TO YOU!
MY STARS! IT'S A BOX OF CHOCOLATES FROM THE WHITEHORSE GENERAL STORE!

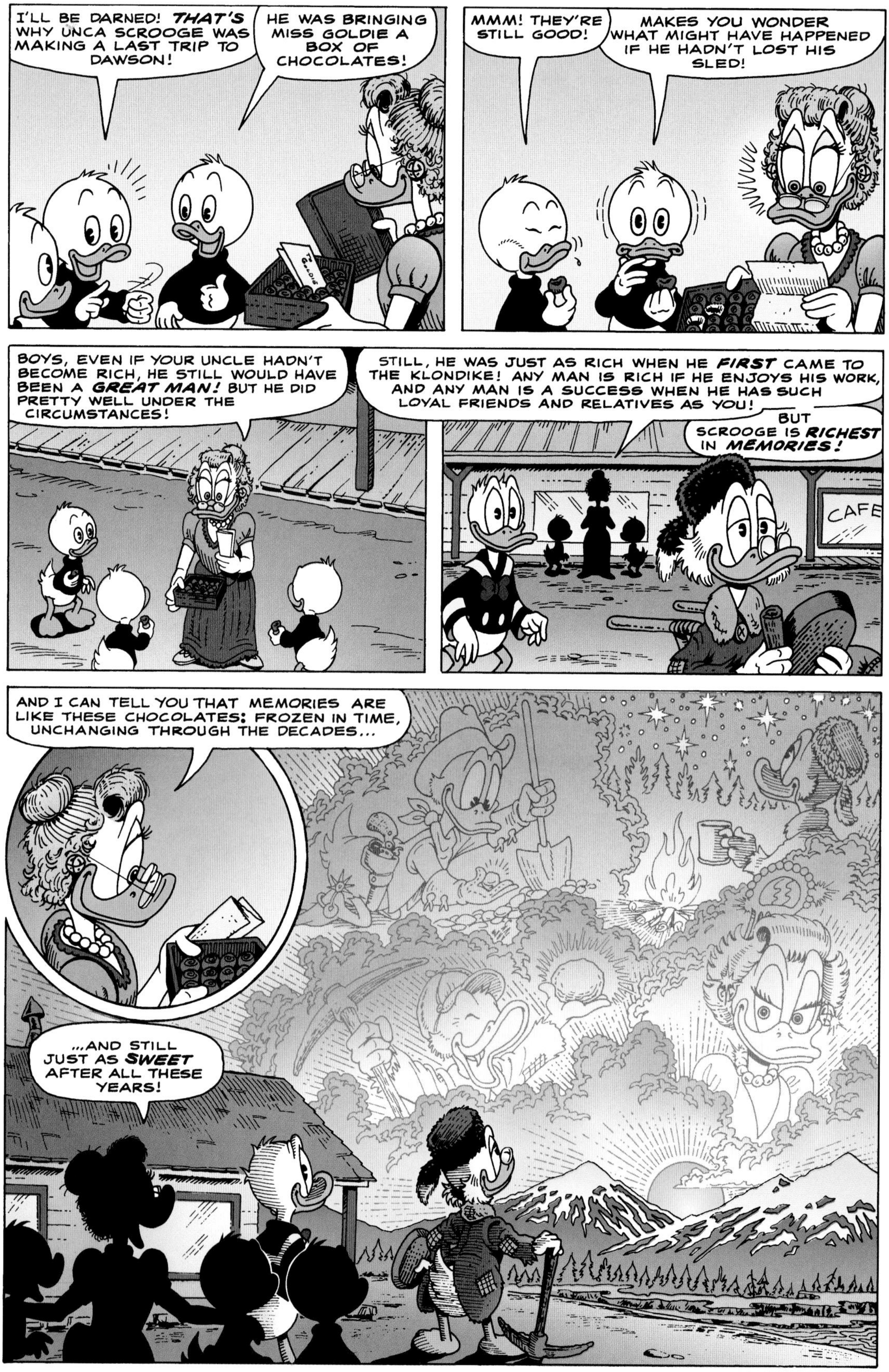
I'LL BE DARNED! THAT'S WHY UNCA SCROOGE WAS MAKING A LAST TRIP TO DAWSON!
HE WAS BRINGING MISS GOLDIE A BOX OF CHOCOLATES!
MMM! THEY'RE STILL GOOD!
MAKES YOU WONDER WHAT MIGHT HAVE HAPPENED IF HE HADN'T LOST HIS SLED!
BOYS, EVEN IF YOUR UNCLE HADN'T BECOME RICH, HE STILL WOULD HAVE BEEN A GREAT MAN! BUT HE DID PRETTY WELL UNDER THE CIRCUMSTANCES!
STILL, HE WAS JUST AS RICH WHEN HE FIRST CAME TO THE KLONDIKE! ANY MAN IS RICH IF HE ENJOYS HIS WORK, AND ANY MAN IS A SUCCESS WHEN HE HAS SUCH LOYAL FRIENDS AND RELATIVES AS YOU!
BUT SCROOGE IS RICHEST IN MEMORIES!
CAFE
AND I CAN TELL YOU THAT MEMORIES ARE LIKE THESE CHOCOLATES: FROZEN IN TIME, UNCHANGING THROUGH THE DECADES...
...AND STILL JUST AS SWEET AFTER ALL THESE YEARS!

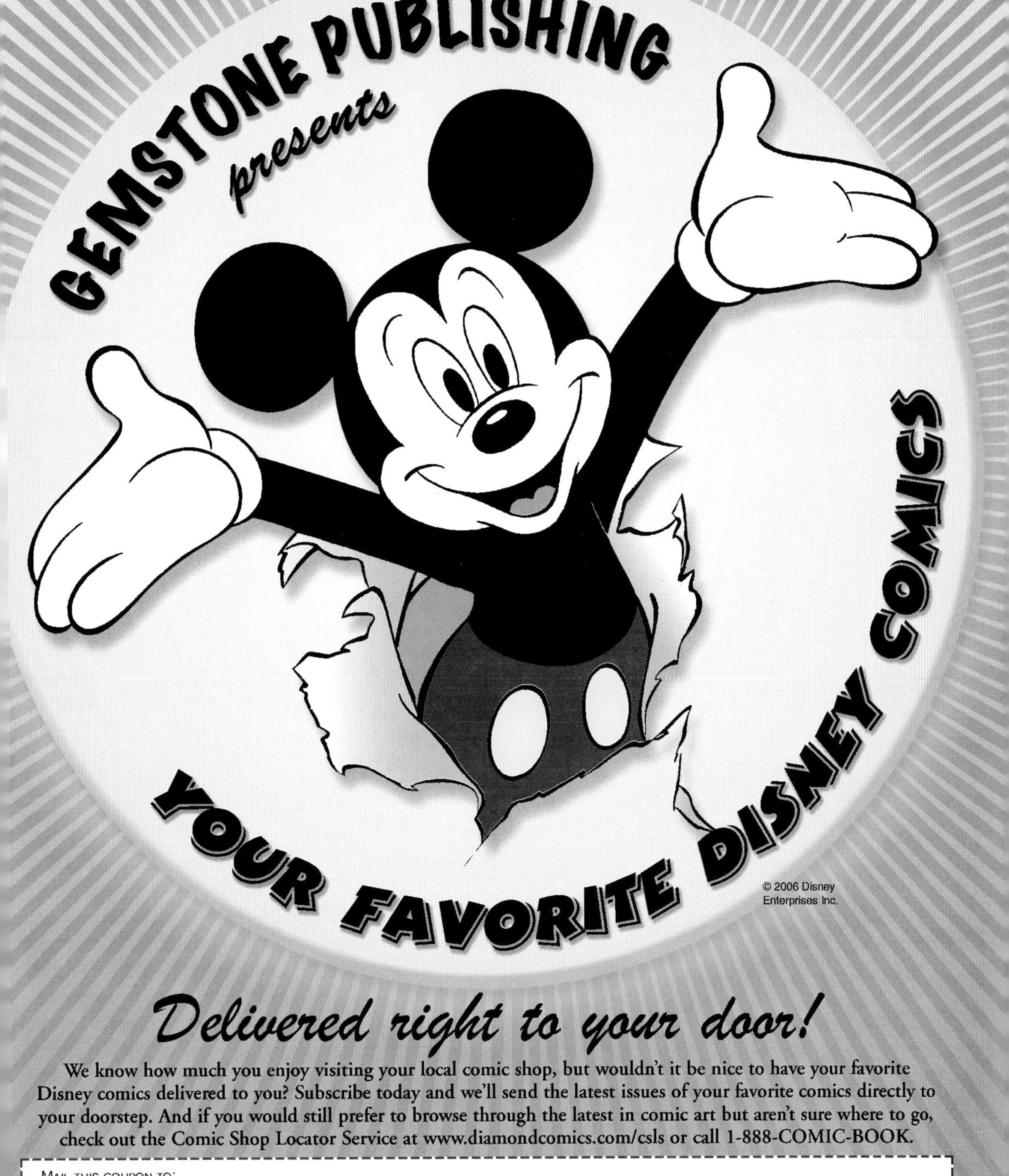
GEMSTONE PUBLISHING
presents
YOUR FAVORITE DISNEY COMICS

Delivered right to your door!

We know how much you enjoy visiting your local comic shop, but wouldn't it be nice to have your favorite Disney comics delivered to you? Subscribe today and we'll send the latest issues of your favorite comics directly to your doorstep. And if you would still prefer to browse through the latest in comic art but aren't sure where to go, check out the Comic Shop Locator Service at www.diamondcomics.com/csls or call 1-888-COMIC-BOOK.

MAIL THIS COUPON TO:

Gemstone Publishing • P.O. Box 469 • West Plains, Missouri 65775

- ☐ ***Walt Disney's Comics & Stories:*** $83.40 for 12 issues, 64 pages ($90.00 Canada, payable in US funds) .... $ ________
- ☐ ***Walt Disney's Donald Duck & Friends:*** $35.40 for 12 issues, 32 pages ($40.00 Canada, payable in US funds) .... $ ________
- ☐ ***Walt Disney's Uncle Scrooge:*** $83.40 for 12 issues, 64 pages ($90.00 Canada, payable in US funds) .... $ ________
- ☐ ***Walt Disney's Mickey Mouse & Friends:*** $35.40 for 12 issues, 32 pages ($40.00 Canada, payable in US funds) .... $ ________
- ☐ ***Donald Duck Adventures:*** $95.40 for 12 bimonthly issues, 128 pages ($105.00 Canada, payable in US funds) .... $ ________
- ☐ ***Mickey Mouse Adventures:*** $95.40 for 12 bimonthly issues, 128 pages ($105.00 Canada, payable in US funds) .... $ ________

SUBTOTAL: $ ________

SALES TAX (MO residents add 6.975% sales tax; MD residents add 5% sales tax): $ ________

TOTAL: $ ________

Name: ____________________

Address: ____________________

____

City: ________ State: ________ Zip: ________

Email: ____________________

CREDIT CARD:

- ☐ Visa
- ☐ MasterCard
- ☐ Other ____________________

Card #: ____________________

Exp. Date: ____________________

SHIVER ME FROZEN TAILFEATHERS!

TWO FROSTY TALES FROM THE SNOWY BADLANDS OF THE YUKON!

GEMSTONE PUBLISHING

$6.95

GEMSTONE PUBLISHING

WALT DISNEY presents

Donald Duck in SOMEWHERE in NOWHERE

Uncle $crooge in NORTH OF THE YUKON

Hop aboard a dogsled bound for adventure as your favorite Disney ducks, Donald and Uncle Scrooge, tangle with some cold-hearted Klondike crooks!

"Somewhere in Nowhere," a unique collaboration between Carl Barks, John Lustig, and Pat Block, marks the last duck adventure on which Barks worked! When Donald tries to get rich in Alaska, the money-making scheme leads to a race against time with the evil Hamalot McSwine!

Then, in Barks' 1965 classic "North of the Yukon," the race is between Scrooge and old-time rival Soapy Slick... with the stakes involving an IOU that could impound the McDuck millions!

Donald Duck and Uncle Scrooge—two feature-length duck epics in one $6.95, 64-page trade paper-back. **Mush,** you huskies!

© 2006 Disney Enterprises Inc.

Walt Disney's Donald Duck

~ Date With A Munchkin ~

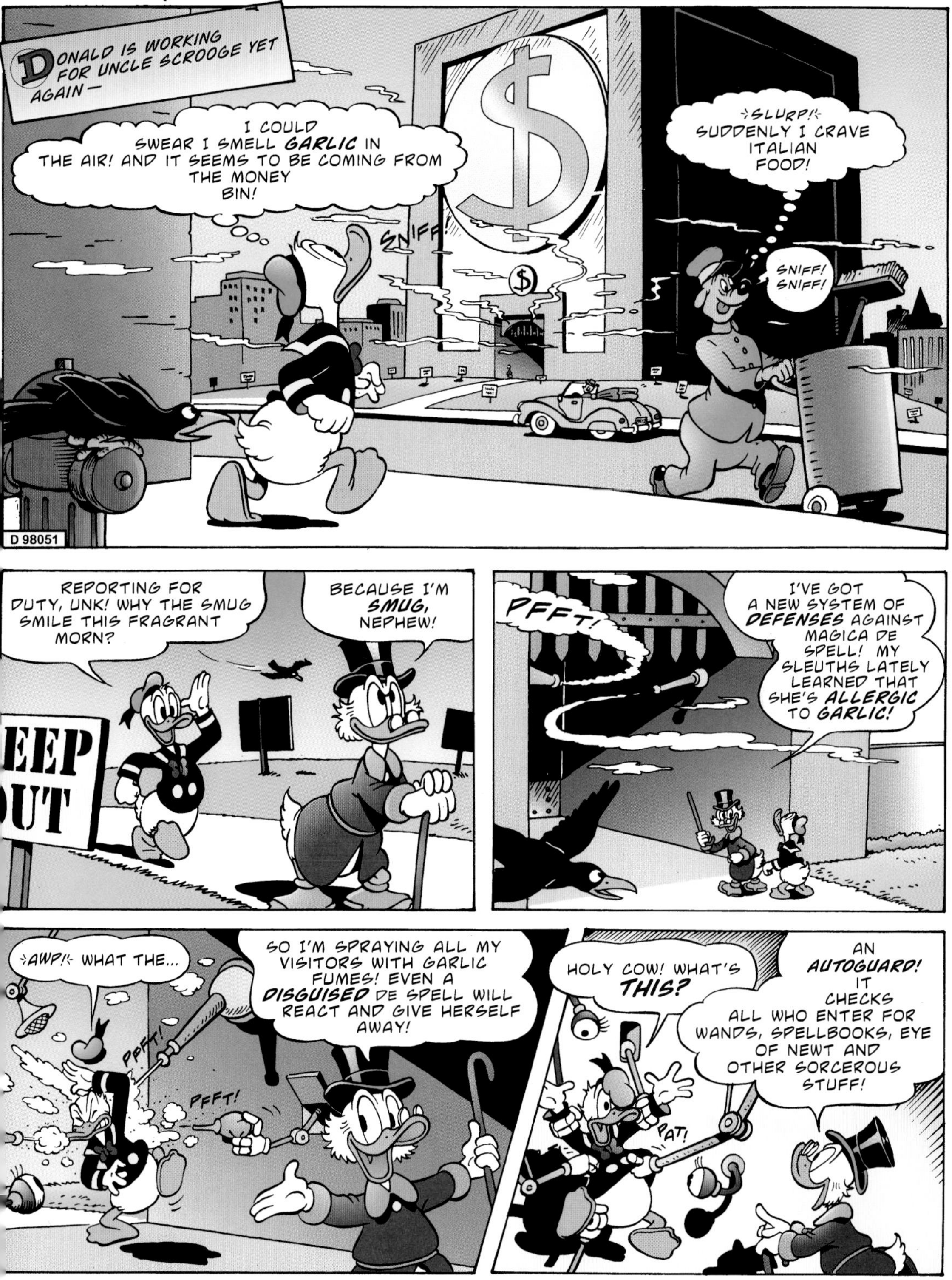
DONALD IS WORKING FOR UNCLE SCROOGE YET AGAIN—
I COULD SWEAR I SMELL GARLIC IN THE AIR! AND IT SEEMS TO BE COMING FROM THE MONEY BIN!
SNIFF
✧SLURP!✧ SUDDENLY I CRAVE ITALIAN FOOD!
SNIFF! SNIFF!
D 98051
REPORTING FOR DUTY, UNK! WHY THE SMUG SMILE THIS FRAGRANT MORN?
BECAUSE I'M SMUG, NEPHEW!
EEP
UT
PFFT!
I'VE GOT A NEW SYSTEM OF DEFENSES AGAINST MAGICA DE SPELL! MY SLEUTHS LATELY LEARNED THAT SHE'S ALLERGIC TO GARLIC!
✧AWP!✧ WHAT THE...
SO I'M SPRAYING ALL MY VISITORS WITH GARLIC FUMES! EVEN A DISGUISED DE SPELL WILL REACT AND GIVE HERSELF AWAY!
PFFT!
PFFT!
HOLY COW! WHAT'S THIS?
AN AUTOGUARD! IT CHECKS ALL WHO ENTER FOR WANDS, SPELLBOOKS, EYE OF NEWT AND OTHER SORCEROUS STUFF!
PAT!

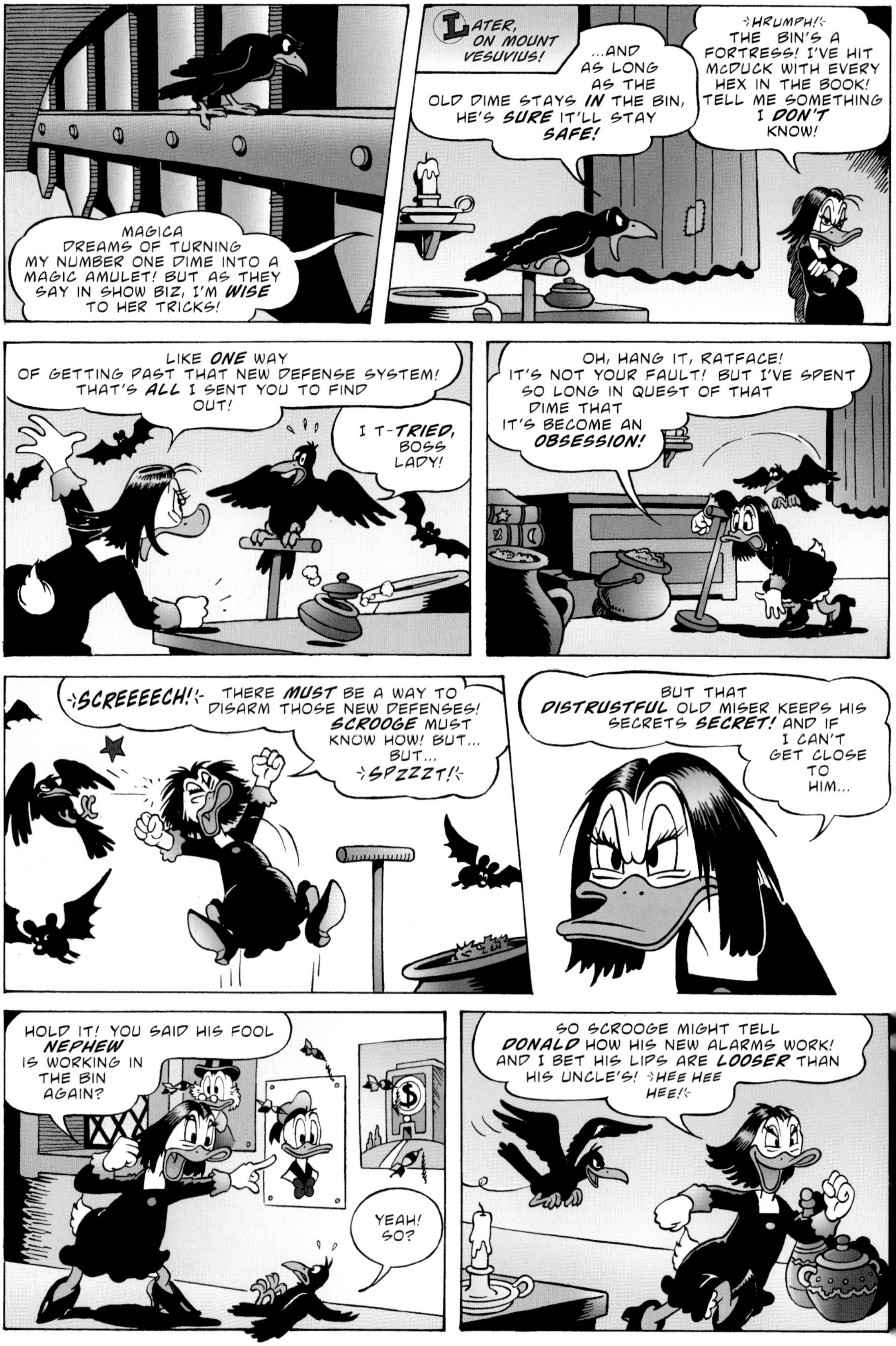
MAGICA DREAMS OF TURNING MY NUMBER ONE DIME INTO A MAGIC AMULET! BUT AS THEY SAY IN SHOW BIZ, I'M WISE TO HER TRICKS!
LATER, ON MOUNT VESUVIUS!
...AND AS LONG AS THE OLD DIME STAYS IN THE BIN, HE'S SURE IT'LL STAY SAFE!
HRUMPH! THE BIN'S A FORTRESS! I'VE HIT McDUCK WITH EVERY HEX IN THE BOOK! TELL ME SOMETHING I DON'T KNOW!
LIKE ONE WAY OF GETTING PAST THAT NEW DEFENSE SYSTEM! THAT'S ALL I SENT YOU TO FIND OUT!
I T-TRIED, BOSS LADY!
OH, HANG IT, RATFACE! IT'S NOT YOUR FAULT! BUT I'VE SPENT SO LONG IN QUEST OF THAT DIME THAT IT'S BECOME AN OBSESSION!
SCREEEECH! THERE MUST BE A WAY TO DISARM THOSE NEW DEFENSES! SCROOGE MUST KNOW HOW! BUT... BUT... SPZZZT!
BUT THAT DISTRUSTFUL OLD MISER KEEPS HIS SECRETS SECRET! AND IF I CAN'T GET CLOSE TO HIM...
HOLD IT! YOU SAID HIS FOOL NEPHEW IS WORKING IN THE BIN AGAIN?
YEAH! SO?
SO SCROOGE MIGHT TELL DONALD HOW HIS NEW ALARMS WORK! AND I BET HIS LIPS ARE LOOSER THAN HIS UNCLE'S! HEE HEE HEE!

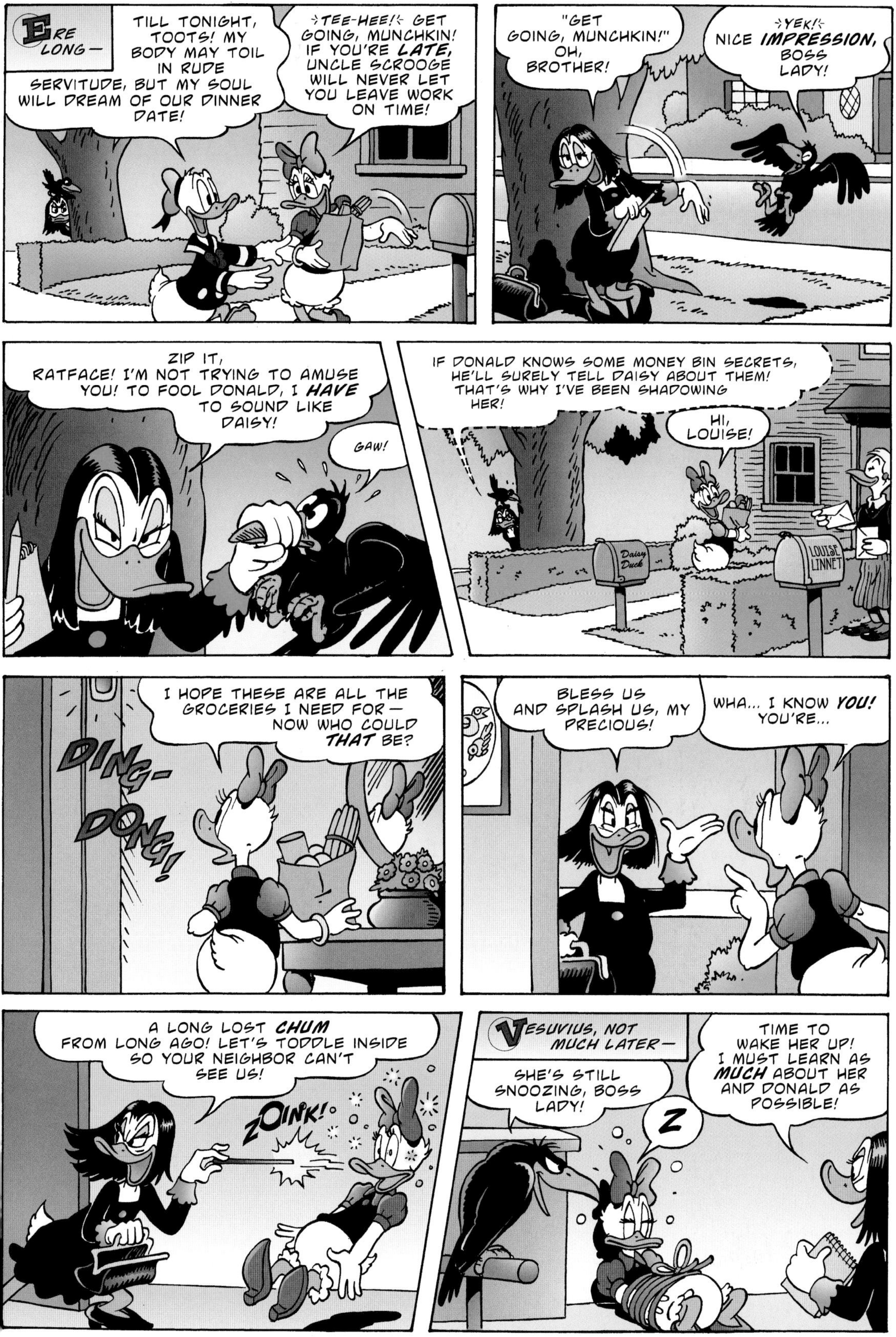
ERE LONG—
TILL TONIGHT, TOOTS! MY BODY MAY TOIL IN RUDE SERVITUDE, BUT MY SOUL WILL DREAM OF OUR DINNER DATE!
✧TEE-HEE!✧ GET GOING, MUNCHKIN! IF YOU'RE LATE, UNCLE SCROOGE WILL NEVER LET YOU LEAVE WORK ON TIME!
"GET GOING, MUNCHKIN!" OH, BROTHER!
✧YEK!✧ NICE IMPRESSION, BOSS LADY!
ZIP IT, RATFACE! I'M NOT TRYING TO AMUSE YOU! TO FOOL DONALD, I HAVE TO SOUND LIKE DAISY!
GAW!
IF DONALD KNOWS SOME MONEY BIN SECRETS, HE'LL SURELY TELL DAISY ABOUT THEM! THAT'S WHY I'VE BEEN SHADOWING HER!
HI, LOUISE!
Daisy Duck
LOUISE LINNET
I HOPE THESE ARE ALL THE GROCERIES I NEED FOR— NOW WHO COULD THAT BE?
DING-DONG!
BLESS US AND SPLASH US, MY PRECIOUS!
WHA... I KNOW YOU! YOU'RE...
A LONG LOST CHUM FROM LONG AGO! LET'S TODDLE INSIDE SO YOUR NEIGHBOR CAN'T SEE US!
ZOINK!
VESUVIUS, NOT MUCH LATER—
SHE'S STILL SNOOZING, BOSS LADY!
Z
TIME TO WAKE HER UP! I MUST LEARN AS MUCH ABOUT HER AND DONALD AS POSSIBLE!

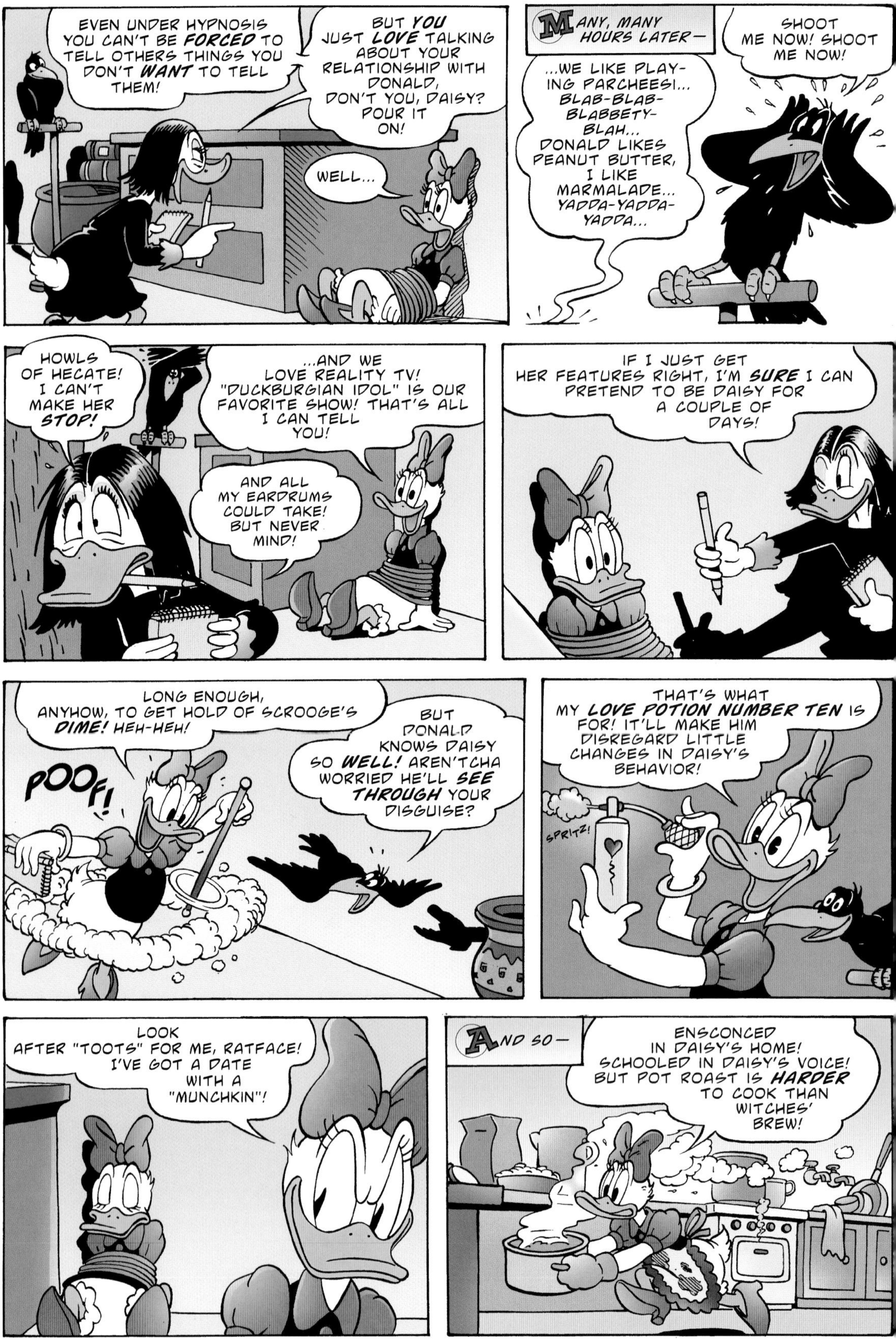
EVEN UNDER HYPNOSIS YOU CAN'T BE **FORCED** TO TELL OTHERS THINGS YOU DON'T **WANT** TO TELL THEM!
BUT **YOU** JUST **LOVE** TALKING ABOUT YOUR RELATIONSHIP WITH DONALD, DON'T YOU, DAISY? POUR IT ON!
WELL...
MANY, MANY HOURS LATER—
...WE LIKE PLAYING PARCHEESI... *BLAB-BLAB-BLABBETY-BLAH...* DONALD LIKES PEANUT BUTTER, I LIKE MARMALADE... *YADDA-YADDA-YADDA...*
SHOOT ME NOW! SHOOT ME NOW!
HOWLS OF HECATE! I CAN'T MAKE HER **STOP!**
...AND WE LOVE REALITY TV! "DUCKBURGIAN IDOL" IS OUR FAVORITE SHOW! THAT'S ALL I CAN TELL YOU!
AND ALL MY EARDRUMS COULD TAKE! BUT NEVER MIND!
IF I JUST GET HER FEATURES RIGHT, I'M **SURE** I CAN PRETEND TO BE DAISY FOR A COUPLE OF DAYS!
LONG ENOUGH, ANYHOW, TO GET HOLD OF SCROOGE'S **DIME!** HEH-HEH!
POOF!
BUT DONALD KNOWS DAISY SO **WELL!** AREN'TCHA WORRIED HE'LL **SEE THROUGH** YOUR DISGUISE?
THAT'S WHAT MY **LOVE POTION NUMBER TEN** IS FOR! IT'LL MAKE HIM DISREGARD LITTLE CHANGES IN DAISY'S BEHAVIOR!
SPRITZ!
LOOK AFTER "TOOTS" FOR ME, RATFACE! I'VE GOT A DATE WITH A "MUNCHKIN"!
AND SO—
ENSCONCED IN DAISY'S HOME! SCHOOLED IN DAISY'S VOICE! BUT POT ROAST IS **HARDER** TO COOK THAN WITCHES' BREW!

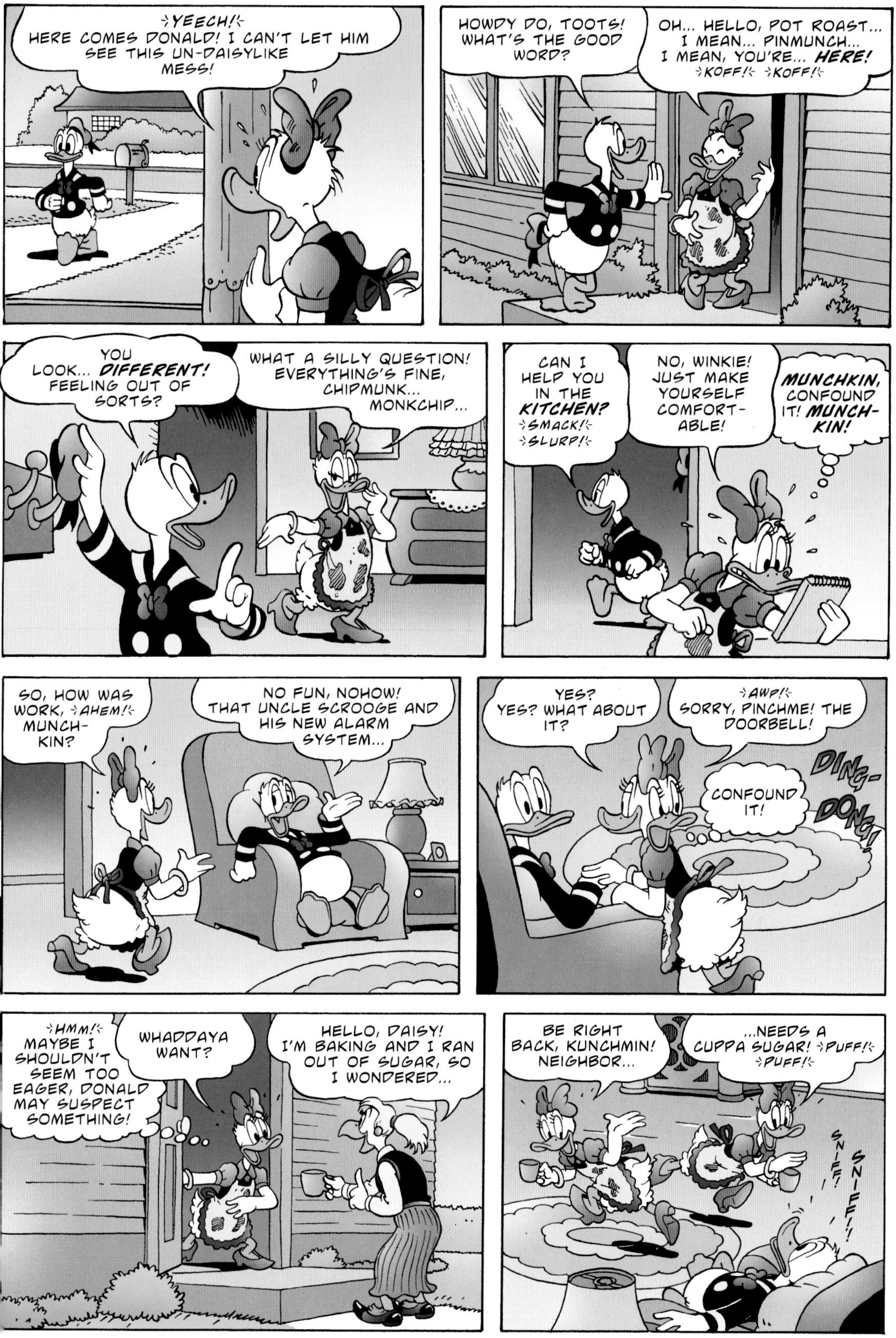
YEECH! HERE COMES DONALD! I CAN'T LET HIM SEE THIS UN-DAISYLIKE MESS!
HOWDY DO, TOOTS! WHAT'S THE GOOD WORD?
OH... HELLO, POT ROAST... I MEAN... PINMUNCH... I MEAN, YOU'RE... HERE! KOFF! KOFF!
YOU LOOK... DIFFERENT! FEELING OUT OF SORTS?
WHAT A SILLY QUESTION! EVERYTHING'S FINE, CHIPMUNK... MONKCHIP...
CAN I HELP YOU IN THE KITCHEN? SMACK! SLURP!
NO, WINKIE! JUST MAKE YOURSELF COMFORTABLE!
MUNCHKIN, CONFOUND IT! MUNCHKIN!
SO, HOW WAS WORK, AHEM! MUNCHKIN?
NO FUN, NOHOW! THAT UNCLE SCROOGE AND HIS NEW ALARM SYSTEM...
YES? YES? WHAT ABOUT IT?
AWP! SORRY, PINCHME! THE DOORBELL!
DING-DONG!
CONFOUND IT!
HMM! MAYBE I SHOULDN'T SEEM TOO EAGER, DONALD MAY SUSPECT SOMETHING!
WHADDAYA WANT?
HELLO, DAISY! I'M BAKING AND I RAN OUT OF SUGAR, SO I WONDERED...
BE RIGHT BACK, KUNCHMIN! NEIGHBOR...
...NEEDS A CUPPA SUGAR! PUFF! PUFF!
SNIFF! SNIFF!!

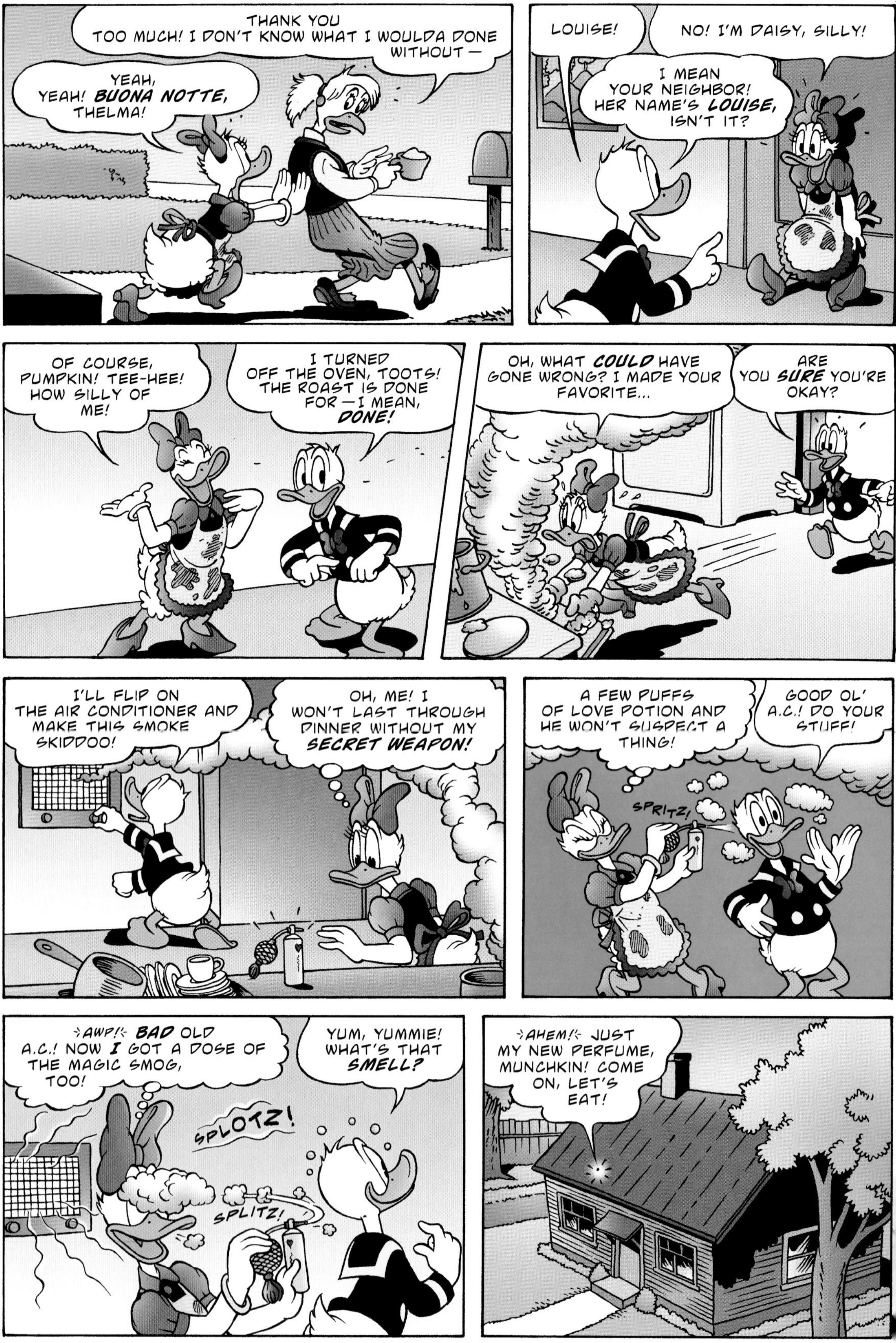
THANK YOU TOO MUCH! I DON'T KNOW WHAT I WOULDA DONE WITHOUT —
YEAH, YEAH! BUONA NOTTE, THELMA!
LOUISE!
NO! I'M DAISY, SILLY!
I MEAN YOUR NEIGHBOR! HER NAME'S LOUISE, ISN'T IT?
OF COURSE, PUMPKIN! TEE-HEE! HOW SILLY OF ME!
I TURNED OFF THE OVEN, TOOTS! THE ROAST IS DONE FOR — I MEAN, DONE!
OH, WHAT COULD HAVE GONE WRONG? I MADE YOUR FAVORITE...
ARE YOU SURE YOU'RE OKAY?
I'LL FLIP ON THE AIR CONDITIONER AND MAKE THIS SMOKE SKIDDOO!
OH, ME! I WON'T LAST THROUGH DINNER WITHOUT MY SECRET WEAPON!
A FEW PUFFS OF LOVE POTION AND HE WON'T SUSPECT A THING!
GOOD OL' A.C.! DO YOUR STUFF!
SPRITZ!
AWP! BAD OLD A.C.! NOW I GOT A DOSE OF THE MAGIC SMOG, TOO!
YUM, YUMMIE! WHAT'S THAT SMELL?
SPLOTZ!
SPLITZ!
AHEM! JUST MY NEW PERFUME, MUNCHKIN! COME ON, LET'S EAT!

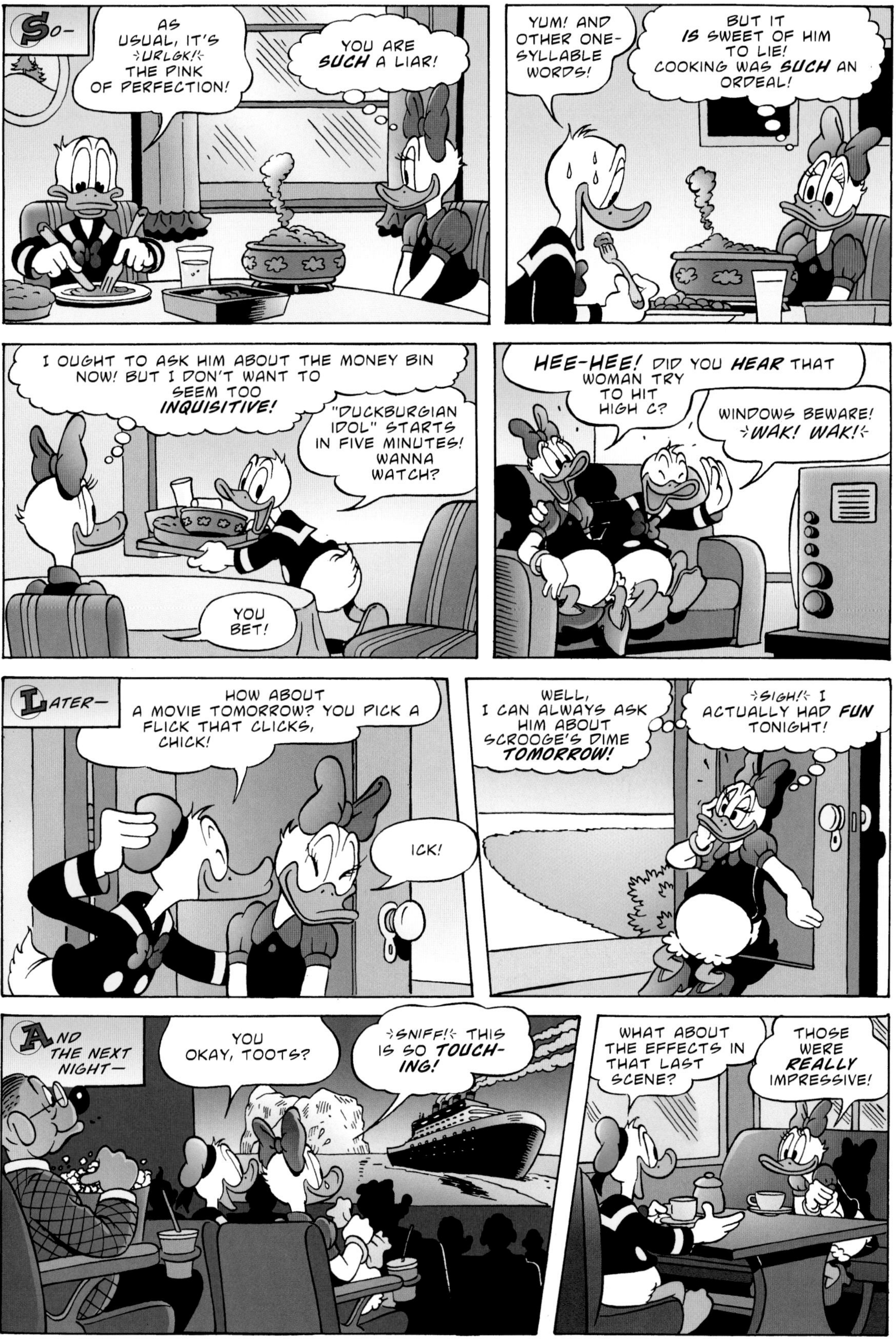
SO—
AS USUAL, IT'S ✧URLGK!✧ THE PINK OF PERFECTION!
YOU ARE SUCH A LIAR!
YUM! AND OTHER ONE-SYLLABLE WORDS!
BUT IT IS SWEET OF HIM TO LIE! COOKING WAS SUCH AN ORDEAL!
I OUGHT TO ASK HIM ABOUT THE MONEY BIN NOW! BUT I DON'T WANT TO SEEM TOO INQUISITIVE!
"DUCKBURGIAN IDOL" STARTS IN FIVE MINUTES! WANNA WATCH?
YOU BET!
HEE-HEE! DID YOU HEAR THAT WOMAN TRY TO HIT HIGH C?
WINDOWS BEWARE! ✧WAK! WAK!✧
LATER—
HOW ABOUT A MOVIE TOMORROW? YOU PICK A FLICK THAT CLICKS, CHICK!
ICK!
WELL, I CAN ALWAYS ASK HIM ABOUT SCROOGE'S DIME TOMORROW!
✧SIGH!✧ I ACTUALLY HAD FUN TONIGHT!
AND THE NEXT NIGHT—
YOU OKAY, TOOTS?
✧SNIFF!✧ THIS IS SO TOUCHING!
WHAT ABOUT THE EFFECTS IN THAT LAST SCENE?
THOSE WERE REALLY IMPRESSIVE!

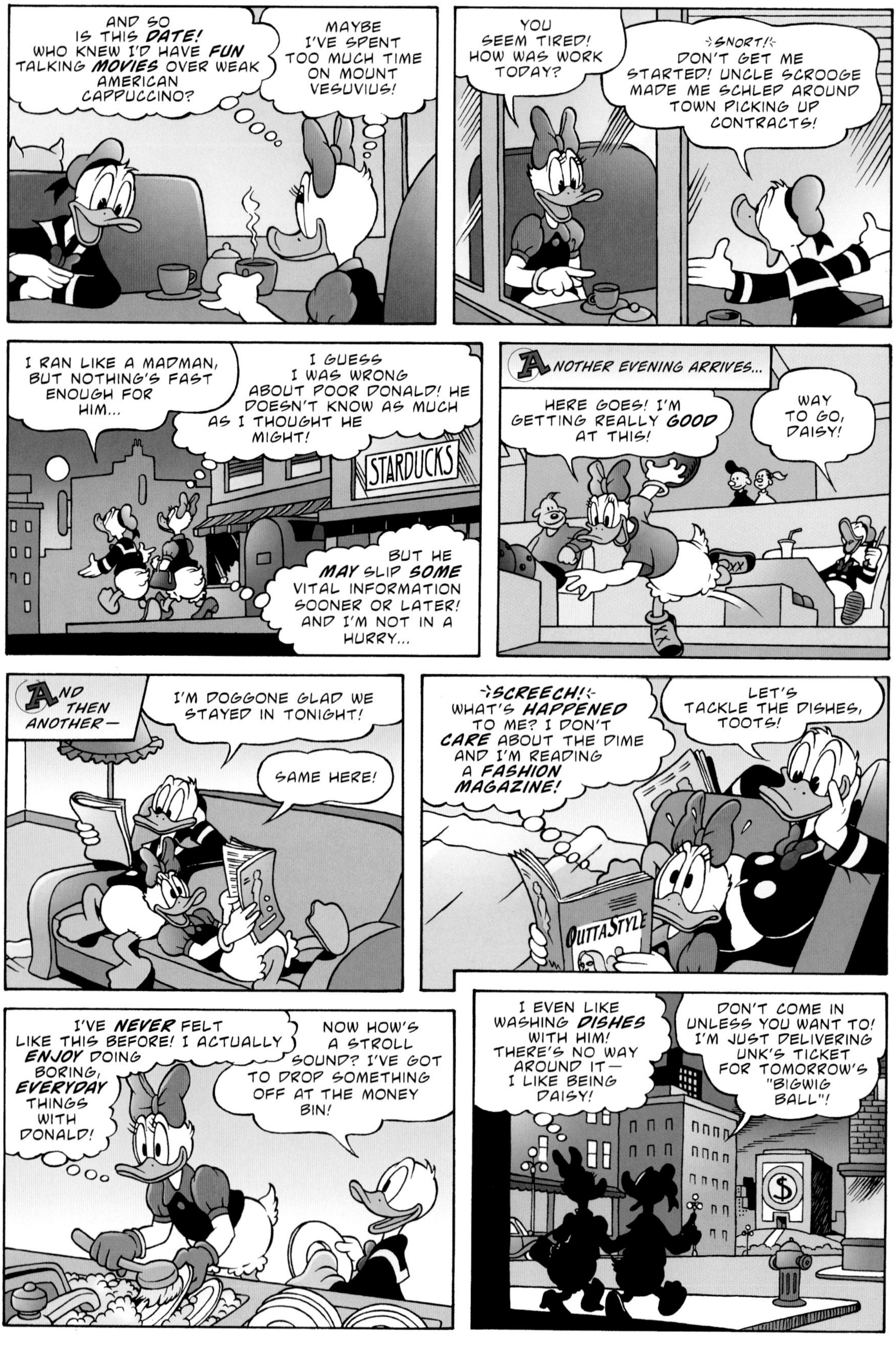
AND SO IS THIS DATE! WHO KNEW I'D HAVE FUN TALKING MOVIES OVER WEAK AMERICAN CAPPUCCINO?
MAYBE I'VE SPENT TOO MUCH TIME ON MOUNT VESUVIUS!
YOU SEEM TIRED! HOW WAS WORK TODAY?
SNORT!
DON'T GET ME STARTED! UNCLE SCROOGE MADE ME SCHLEP AROUND TOWN PICKING UP CONTRACTS!
I RAN LIKE A MADMAN, BUT NOTHING'S FAST ENOUGH FOR HIM...
I GUESS I WAS WRONG ABOUT POOR DONALD! HE DOESN'T KNOW AS MUCH AS I THOUGHT HE MIGHT!
STARDUCKS
BUT HE MAY SLIP SOME VITAL INFORMATION SOONER OR LATER! AND I'M NOT IN A HURRY...
ANOTHER EVENING ARRIVES...
HERE GOES! I'M GETTING REALLY GOOD AT THIS!
WAY TO GO, DAISY!
AND THEN ANOTHER—
I'M DOGGONE GLAD WE STAYED IN TONIGHT!
SAME HERE!
SCREECH!
WHAT'S HAPPENED TO ME? I DON'T CARE ABOUT THE DIME AND I'M READING A FASHION MAGAZINE!
LET'S TACKLE THE DISHES, TOOTS!
OUTTASTYLE
I'VE NEVER FELT LIKE THIS BEFORE! I ACTUALLY ENJOY DOING BORING, EVERYDAY THINGS WITH DONALD!
NOW HOW'S A STROLL SOUND? I'VE GOT TO DROP SOMETHING OFF AT THE MONEY BIN!
I EVEN LIKE WASHING DISHES WITH HIM! THERE'S NO WAY AROUND IT— I LIKE BEING DAISY!
DON'T COME IN UNLESS YOU WANT TO! I'M JUST DELIVERING UNK'S TICKET FOR TOMORROW'S "BIGWIG BALL"!

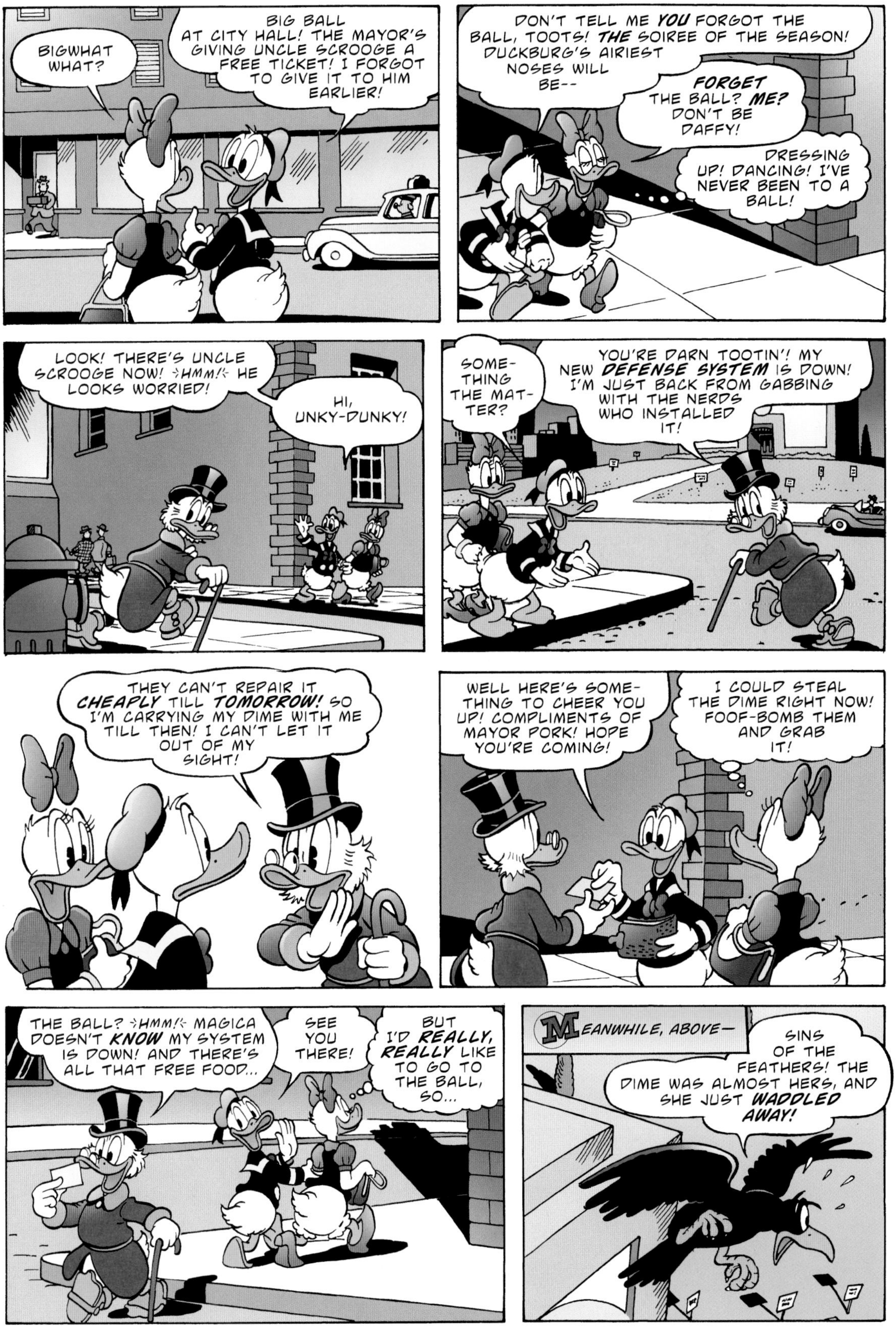
BIGWHAT WHAT?
BIG BALL AT CITY HALL! THE MAYOR'S GIVING UNCLE SCROOGE A FREE TICKET! I FORGOT TO GIVE IT TO HIM EARLIER!
DON'T TELL ME YOU FORGOT THE BALL, TOOTS! THE SOIREE OF THE SEASON! DUCKBURG'S AIRIEST NOSES WILL BE--
FORGET THE BALL? ME? DON'T BE DAFFY!
DRESSING UP! DANCING! I'VE NEVER BEEN TO A BALL!
LOOK! THERE'S UNCLE SCROOGE NOW! HMM! HE LOOKS WORRIED!
HI, UNKY-DUNKY!
SOME-THING THE MAT-TER?
YOU'RE DARN TOOTIN'! MY NEW DEFENSE SYSTEM IS DOWN! I'M JUST BACK FROM GABBING WITH THE NERDS WHO INSTALLED IT!
THEY CAN'T REPAIR IT CHEAPLY TILL TOMORROW! SO I'M CARRYING MY DIME WITH ME TILL THEN! I CAN'T LET IT OUT OF MY SIGHT!
WELL HERE'S SOME-THING TO CHEER YOU UP! COMPLIMENTS OF MAYOR PORK! HOPE YOU'RE COMING!
I COULD STEAL THE DIME RIGHT NOW! FOOF-BOMB THEM AND GRAB IT!
THE BALL? HMM! MAGICA DOESN'T KNOW MY SYSTEM IS DOWN! AND THERE'S ALL THAT FREE FOOD...
SEE YOU THERE!
BUT I'D REALLY, REALLY LIKE TO GO TO THE BALL, SO...
MEANWHILE, ABOVE—
SINS OF THE FEATHERS! THE DIME WAS ALMOST HERS, AND SHE JUST WADDLED AWAY!

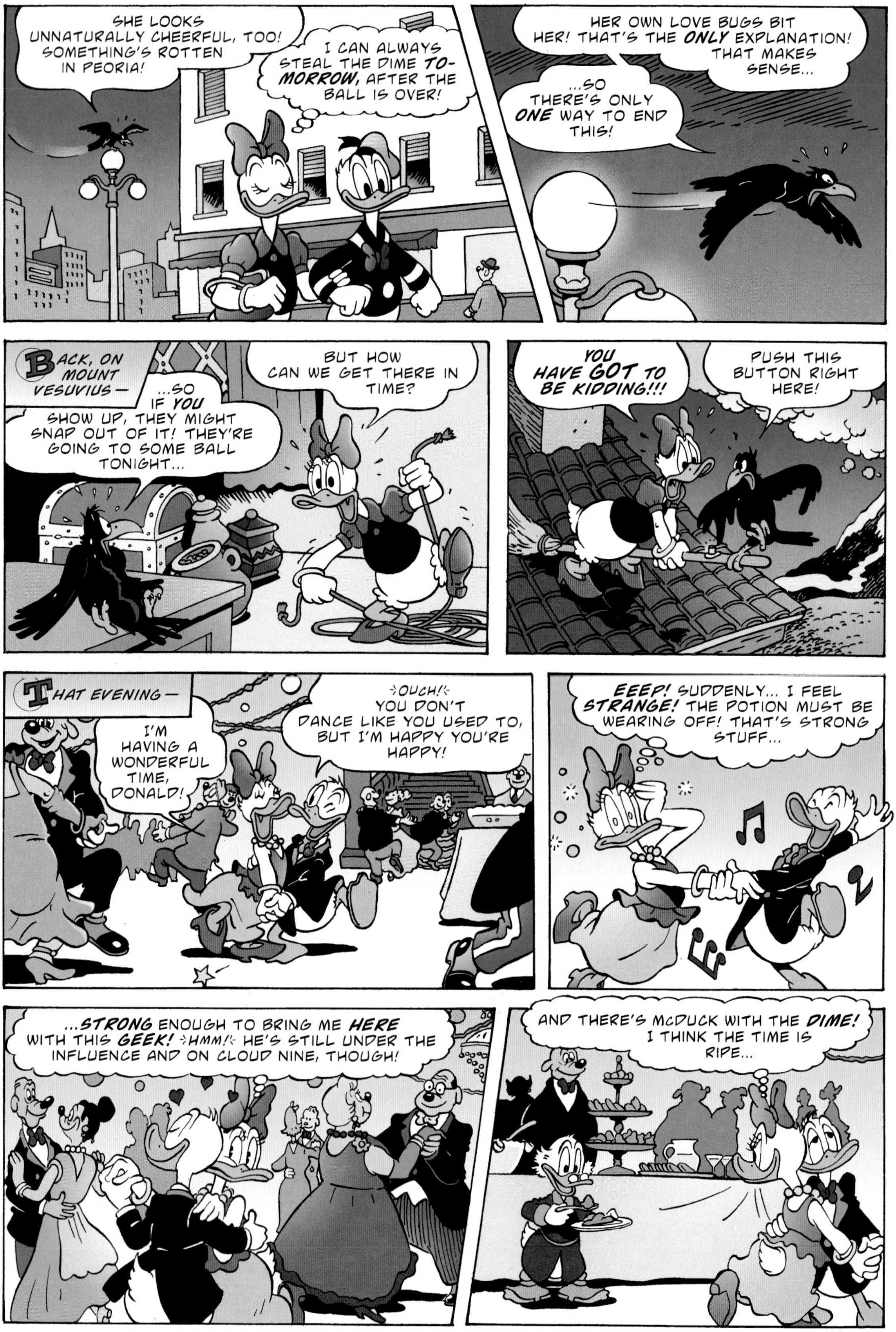
SHE LOOKS UNNATURALLY CHEERFUL, TOO! SOMETHING'S ROTTEN IN PEORIA!
I CAN ALWAYS STEAL THE DIME TO-MORROW, AFTER THE BALL IS OVER!
HER OWN LOVE BUGS BIT HER! THAT'S THE ONLY EXPLANATION! THAT MAKES SENSE...
...SO THERE'S ONLY ONE WAY TO END THIS!
BACK, ON MOUNT VESUVIUS—
...SO IF YOU SHOW UP, THEY MIGHT SNAP OUT OF IT! THEY'RE GOING TO SOME BALL TONIGHT...
BUT HOW CAN WE GET THERE IN TIME?
YOU HAVE GOT TO BE KIDDING!!!
PUSH THIS BUTTON RIGHT HERE!
THAT EVENING—
I'M HAVING A WONDERFUL TIME, DONALD!
OUCH! YOU DON'T DANCE LIKE YOU USED TO, BUT I'M HAPPY YOU'RE HAPPY!
EEEP! SUDDENLY... I FEEL STRANGE! THE POTION MUST BE WEARING OFF! THAT'S STRONG STUFF...
...STRONG ENOUGH TO BRING ME HERE WITH THIS GEEK! HMM! HE'S STILL UNDER THE INFLUENCE AND ON CLOUD NINE, THOUGH!
AND THERE'S McDUCK WITH THE DIME! I THINK THE TIME IS RIPE...

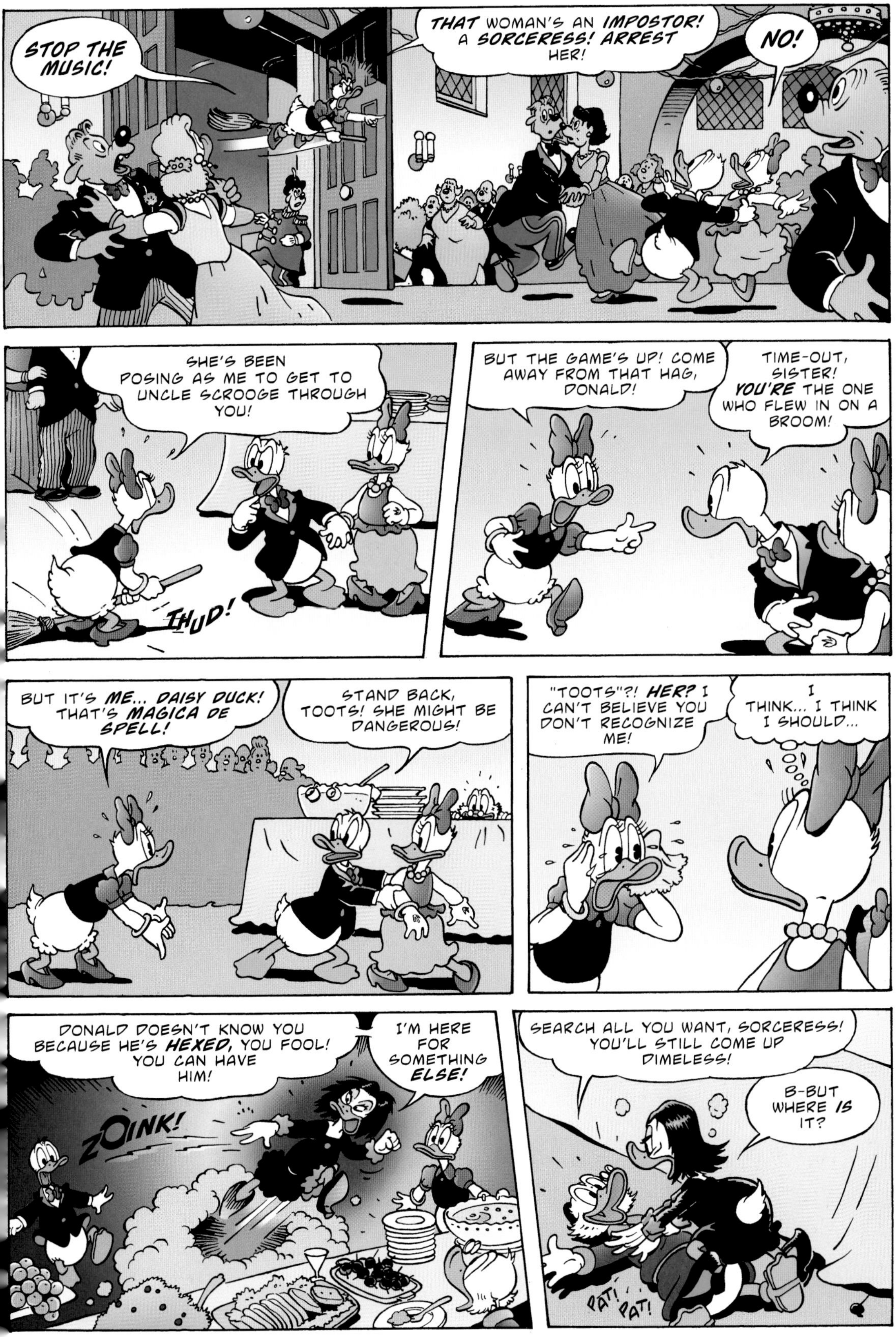
STOP THE MUSIC!
THAT WOMAN'S AN IMPOSTOR! A SORCERESS! ARREST HER!
NO!
SHE'S BEEN POSING AS ME TO GET TO UNCLE SCROOGE THROUGH YOU!
THUD!
BUT THE GAME'S UP! COME AWAY FROM THAT HAG, DONALD!
TIME-OUT, SISTER! YOU'RE THE ONE WHO FLEW IN ON A BROOM!
BUT IT'S ME... DAISY DUCK! THAT'S MAGICA DE SPELL!
STAND BACK, TOOTS! SHE MIGHT BE DANGEROUS!
"TOOTS"?! HER? I CAN'T BELIEVE YOU DON'T RECOGNIZE ME!
I THINK... I THINK I SHOULD...
DONALD DOESN'T KNOW YOU BECAUSE HE'S HEXED, YOU FOOL! YOU CAN HAVE HIM!
I'M HERE FOR SOMETHING ELSE!
ZOINK!
SEARCH ALL YOU WANT, SORCERESS! YOU'LL STILL COME UP DIMELESS!
B-BUT WHERE IS IT?
PAT! PAT!

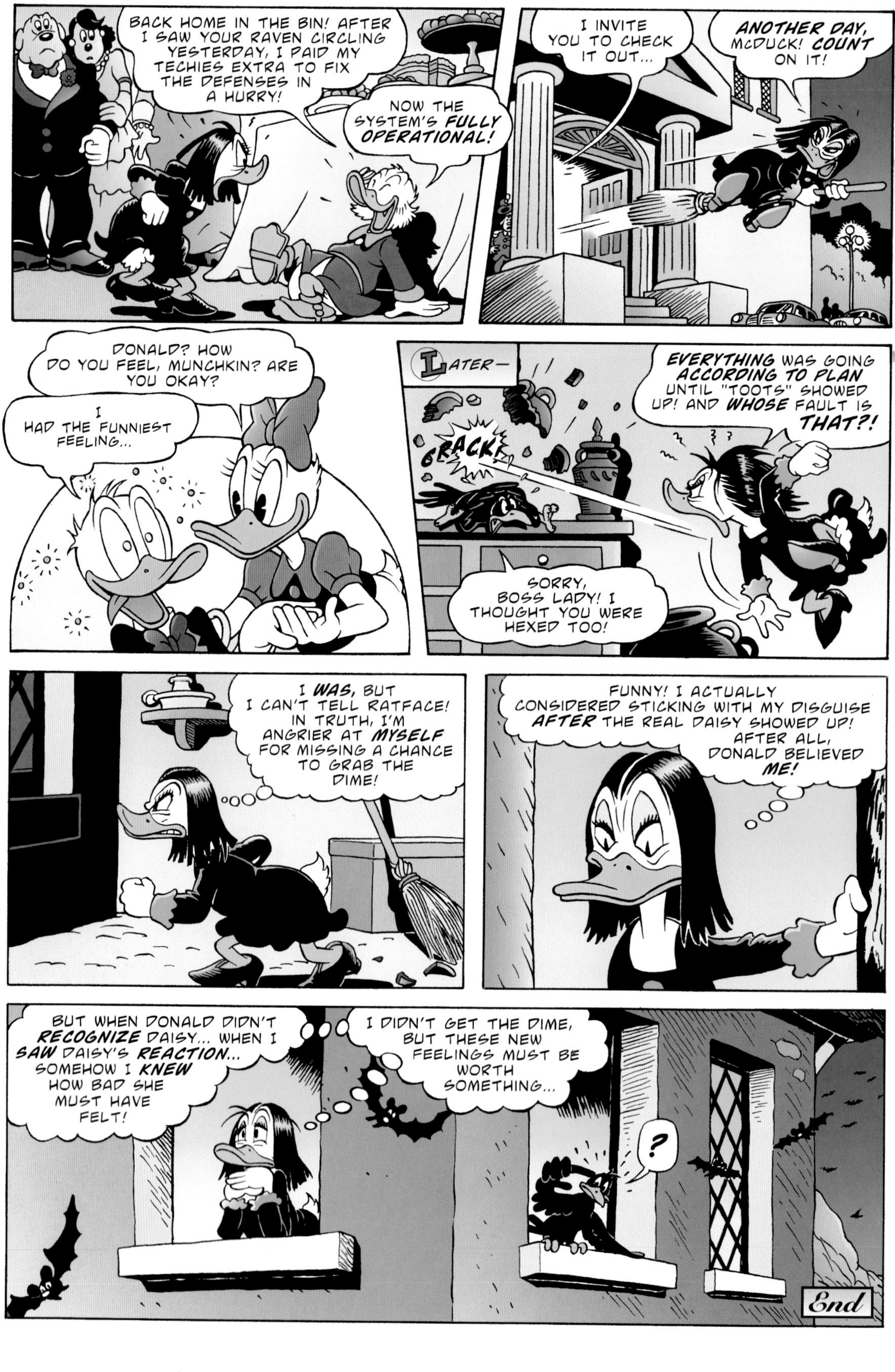
BACK HOME IN THE BIN! AFTER I SAW YOUR RAVEN CIRCLING YESTERDAY, I PAID MY TECHIES EXTRA TO FIX THE DEFENSES IN A HURRY!
NOW THE SYSTEM'S FULLY OPERATIONAL!
I INVITE YOU TO CHECK IT OUT...
ANOTHER DAY, McDUCK! COUNT ON IT!
DONALD? HOW DO YOU FEEL, MUNCHKIN? ARE YOU OKAY?
I HAD THE FUNNIEST FEELING...
LATER—
EVERYTHING WAS GOING ACCORDING TO PLAN UNTIL "TOOTS" SHOWED UP! AND WHOSE FAULT IS THAT?!
CRACK!
SORRY, BOSS LADY! I THOUGHT YOU WERE HEXED TOO!
I WAS, BUT I CAN'T TELL RATFACE! IN TRUTH, I'M ANGRIER AT MYSELF FOR MISSING A CHANCE TO GRAB THE DIME!
FUNNY! I ACTUALLY CONSIDERED STICKING WITH MY DISGUISE AFTER THE REAL DAISY SHOWED UP! AFTER ALL, DONALD BELIEVED ME!
BUT WHEN DONALD DIDN'T RECOGNIZE DAISY... WHEN I SAW DAISY'S REACTION... SOMEHOW I KNEW HOW BAD SHE MUST HAVE FELT!
I DIDN'T GET THE DIME, BUT THESE NEW FEELINGS MUST BE WORTH SOMETHING...
?
End

Walt Disney's The Beagle Boys in Lovestruck Lugs

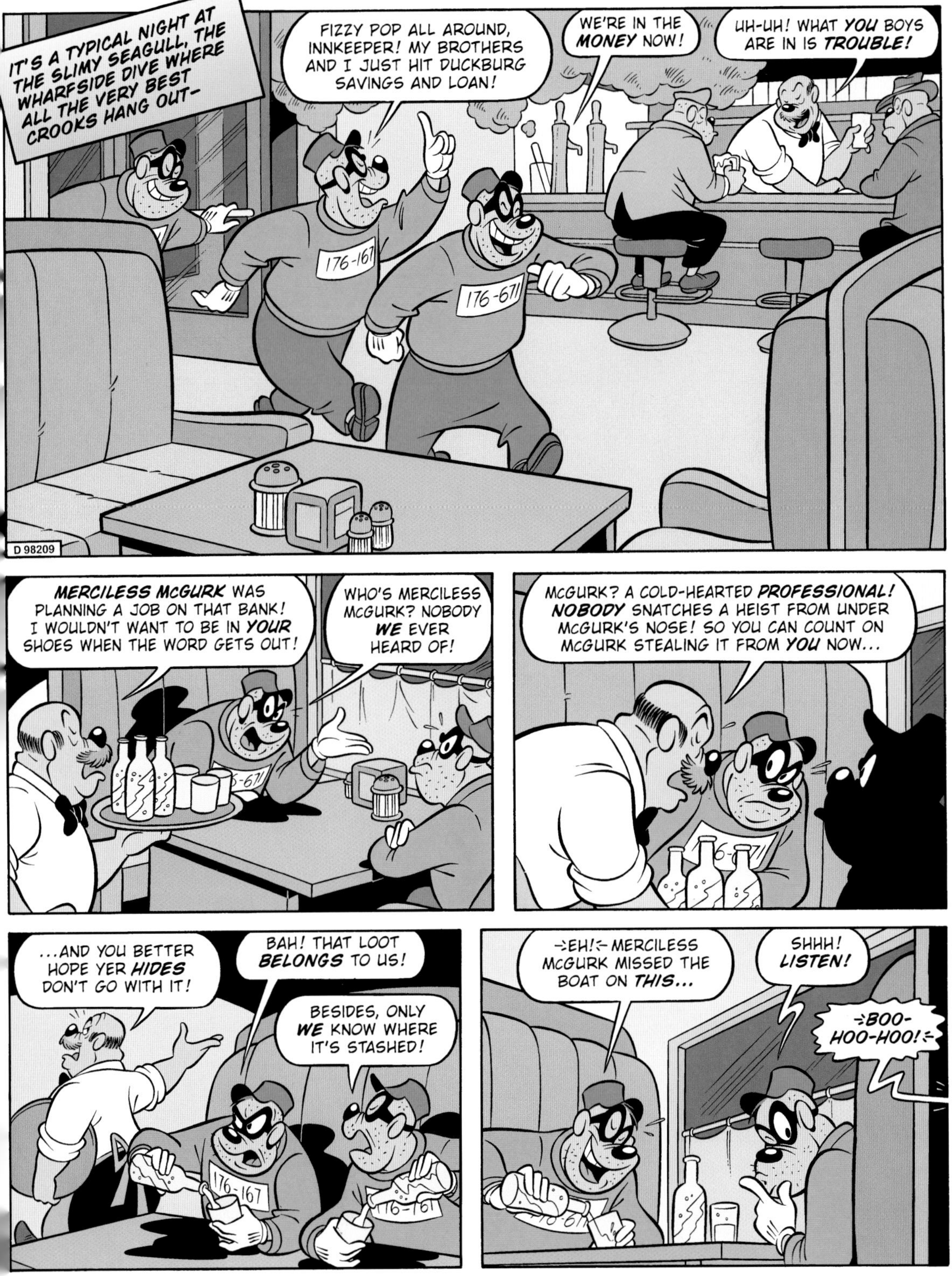

IT'S A TYPICAL NIGHT AT THE SLIMY SEAGULL, THE WHARFSIDE DIVE WHERE ALL THE VERY BEST CROOKS HANG OUT–
FIZZY POP ALL AROUND, INNKEEPER! MY BROTHERS AND I JUST HIT DUCKBURG SAVINGS AND LOAN!
WE'RE IN THE MONEY NOW!
UH-UH! WHAT YOU BOYS ARE IN IS TROUBLE!
176-167
176-671
D 98209
MERCILESS McGURK WAS PLANNING A JOB ON THAT BANK! I WOULDN'T WANT TO BE IN YOUR SHOES WHEN THE WORD GETS OUT!
WHO'S MERCILESS McGURK? NOBODY WE EVER HEARD OF!
McGURK? A COLD-HEARTED PROFESSIONAL! NOBODY SNATCHES A HEIST FROM UNDER McGURK'S NOSE! SO YOU CAN COUNT ON McGURK STEALING IT FROM YOU NOW...
...AND YOU BETTER HOPE YER HIDES DON'T GO WITH IT!
BAH! THAT LOOT BELONGS TO US!
BESIDES, ONLY WE KNOW WHERE IT'S STASHED!
176-167
EH! MERCILESS McGURK MISSED THE BOAT ON THIS...
SHHH! LISTEN!
BOO-HOO-HOO!

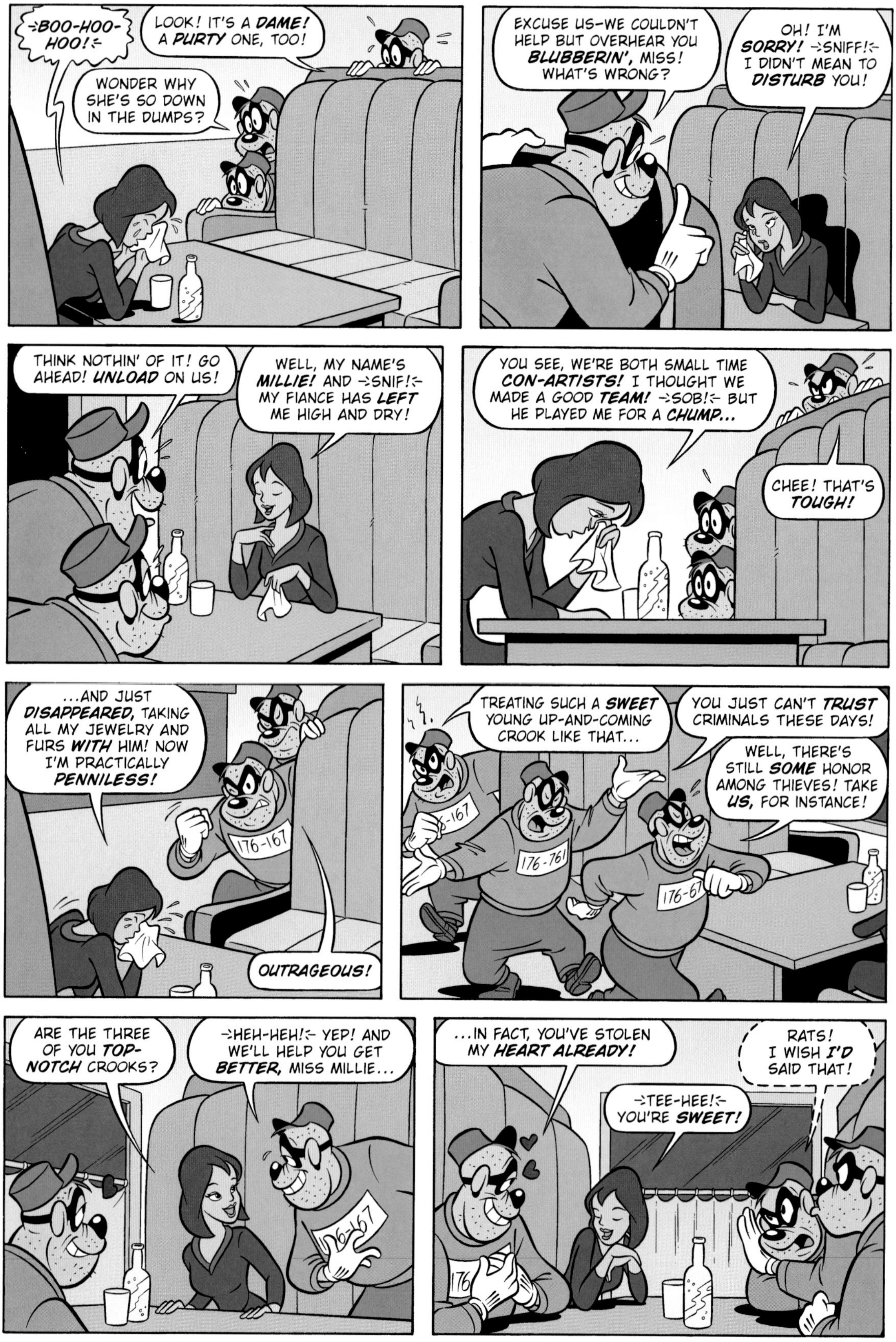
→BOO-HOO-HOO!←
LOOK! IT'S A DAME! A PURTY ONE, TOO!
WONDER WHY SHE'S SO DOWN IN THE DUMPS?
EXCUSE US–WE COULDN'T HELP BUT OVERHEAR YOU BLUBBERIN', MISS! WHAT'S WRONG?
OH! I'M SORRY! →SNIFF!← I DIDN'T MEAN TO DISTURB YOU!
THINK NOTHIN' OF IT! GO AHEAD! UNLOAD ON US!
WELL, MY NAME'S MILLIE! AND →SNIF!← MY FIANCE HAS LEFT ME HIGH AND DRY!
YOU SEE, WE'RE BOTH SMALL TIME CON-ARTISTS! I THOUGHT WE MADE A GOOD TEAM! →SOB!← BUT HE PLAYED ME FOR A CHUMP...
CHEE! THAT'S TOUGH!
...AND JUST DISAPPEARED, TAKING ALL MY JEWELRY AND FURS WITH HIM! NOW I'M PRACTICALLY PENNILESS!
176-167
OUTRAGEOUS!
TREATING SUCH A SWEET YOUNG UP-AND-COMING CROOK LIKE THAT...
YOU JUST CAN'T TRUST CRIMINALS THESE DAYS!
WELL, THERE'S STILL SOME HONOR AMONG THIEVES! TAKE US, FOR INSTANCE!
176-761
ARE THE THREE OF YOU TOP-NOTCH CROOKS?
→HEH-HEH!← YEP! AND WE'LL HELP YOU GET BETTER, MISS MILLIE...
176-167
...IN FACT, YOU'VE STOLEN MY HEART ALREADY!
→TEE-HEE!← YOU'RE SWEET!
RATS! I WISH I'D SAID THAT!

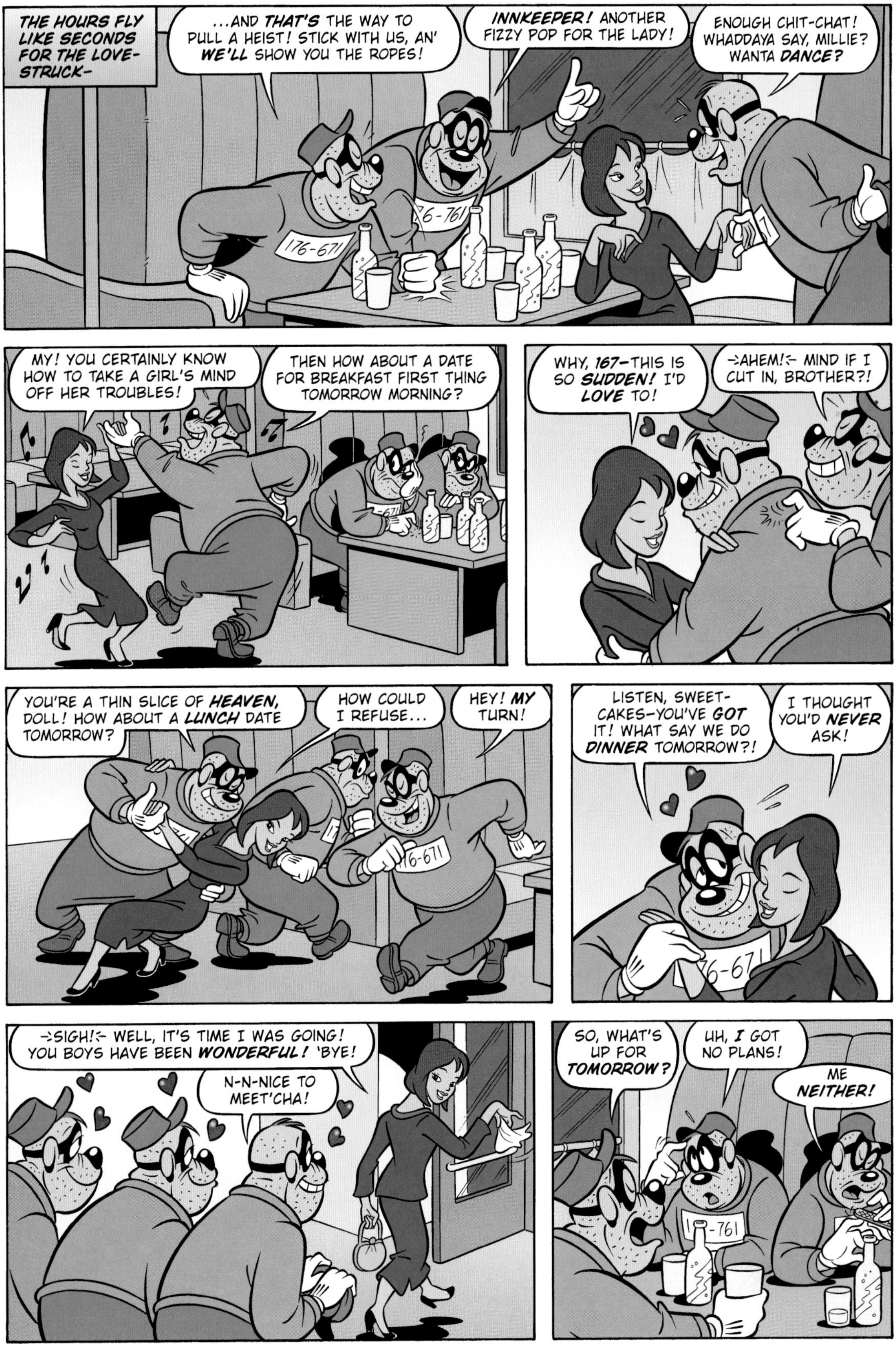
THE HOURS FLY LIKE SECONDS FOR THE LOVE-STRUCK–
...AND THAT'S THE WAY TO PULL A HEIST! STICK WITH US, AN' WE'LL SHOW YOU THE ROPES!
INNKEEPER! ANOTHER FIZZY POP FOR THE LADY!
ENOUGH CHIT-CHAT! WHADDAYA SAY, MILLIE? WANTA DANCE?
176-671
MY! YOU CERTAINLY KNOW HOW TO TAKE A GIRL'S MIND OFF HER TROUBLES!
THEN HOW ABOUT A DATE FOR BREAKFAST FIRST THING TOMORROW MORNING?
WHY, 167–THIS IS SO SUDDEN! I'D LOVE TO!
–AHEM!– MIND IF I CUT IN, BROTHER?!
YOU'RE A THIN SLICE OF HEAVEN, DOLL! HOW ABOUT A LUNCH DATE TOMORROW?
HOW COULD I REFUSE...
HEY! MY TURN!
LISTEN, SWEET-CAKES–YOU'VE GOT IT! WHAT SAY WE DO DINNER TOMORROW?!
I THOUGHT YOU'D NEVER ASK!
–SIGH!– WELL, IT'S TIME I WAS GOING! YOU BOYS HAVE BEEN WONDERFUL! 'BYE!
N-N-NICE TO MEET'CHA!
SO, WHAT'S UP FOR TOMORROW?
UH, I GOT NO PLANS!
ME NEITHER!

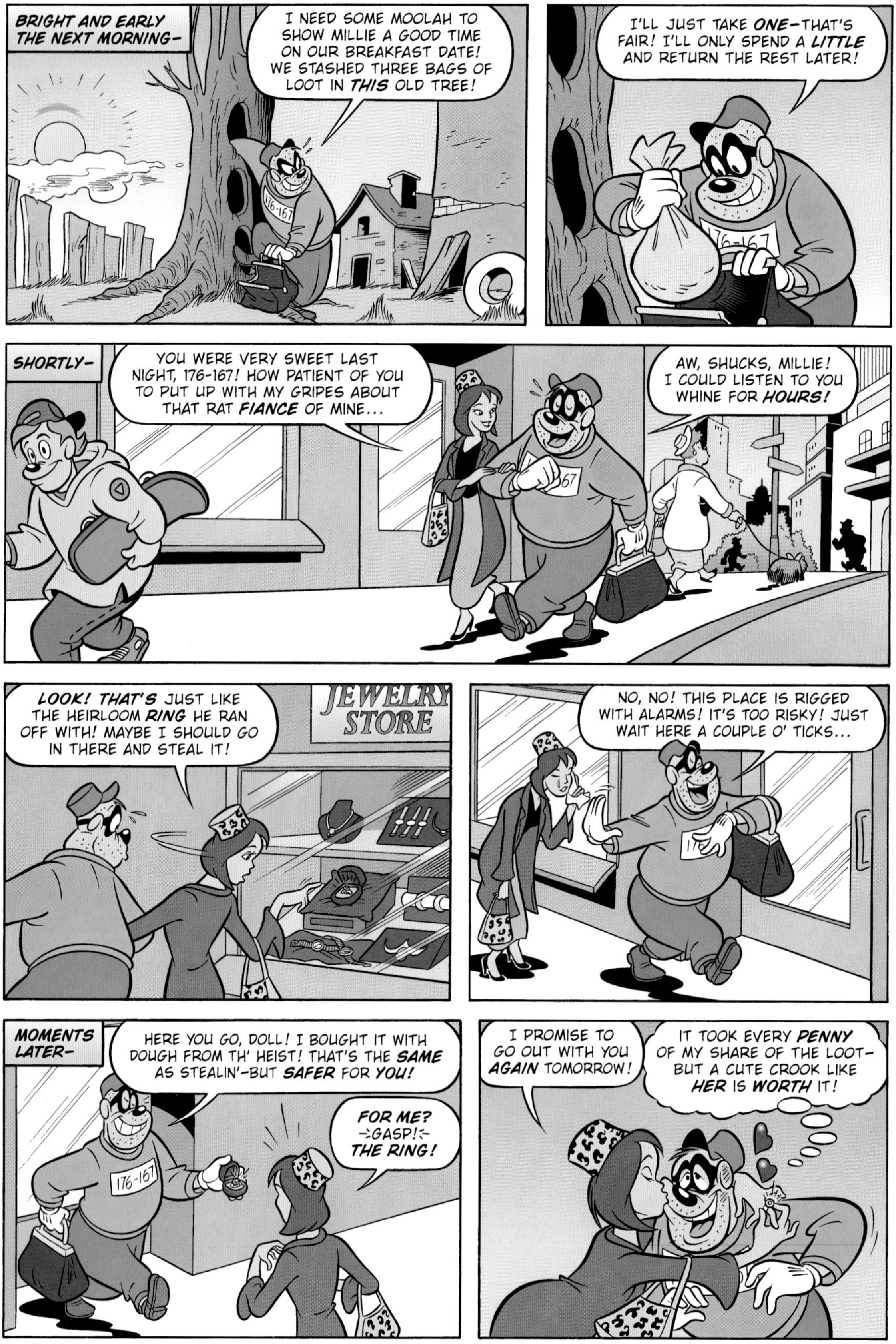
BRIGHT AND EARLY THE NEXT MORNING–
I NEED SOME MOOLAH TO SHOW MILLIE A GOOD TIME ON OUR BREAKFAST DATE! WE STASHED THREE BAGS OF LOOT IN THIS OLD TREE!
176-167
I'LL JUST TAKE ONE–THAT'S FAIR! I'LL ONLY SPEND A LITTLE AND RETURN THE REST LATER!
176-167
SHORTLY–
YOU WERE VERY SWEET LAST NIGHT, 176-167! HOW PATIENT OF YOU TO PUT UP WITH MY GRIPES ABOUT THAT RAT FIANCE OF MINE...
AW, SHUCKS, MILLIE! I COULD LISTEN TO YOU WHINE FOR HOURS!
LOOK! THAT'S JUST LIKE THE HEIRLOOM RING HE RAN OFF WITH! MAYBE I SHOULD GO IN THERE AND STEAL IT!
JEWELRY STORE
NO, NO! THIS PLACE IS RIGGED WITH ALARMS! IT'S TOO RISKY! JUST WAIT HERE A COUPLE O' TICKS...
MOMENTS LATER–
HERE YOU GO, DOLL! I BOUGHT IT WITH DOUGH FROM TH' HEIST! THAT'S THE SAME AS STEALIN'–BUT SAFER FOR YOU!
176-167
FOR ME? –GASP!– THE RING!
I PROMISE TO GO OUT WITH YOU AGAIN TOMORROW!
IT TOOK EVERY PENNY OF MY SHARE OF THE LOOT–BUT A CUTE CROOK LIKE HER IS WORTH IT!

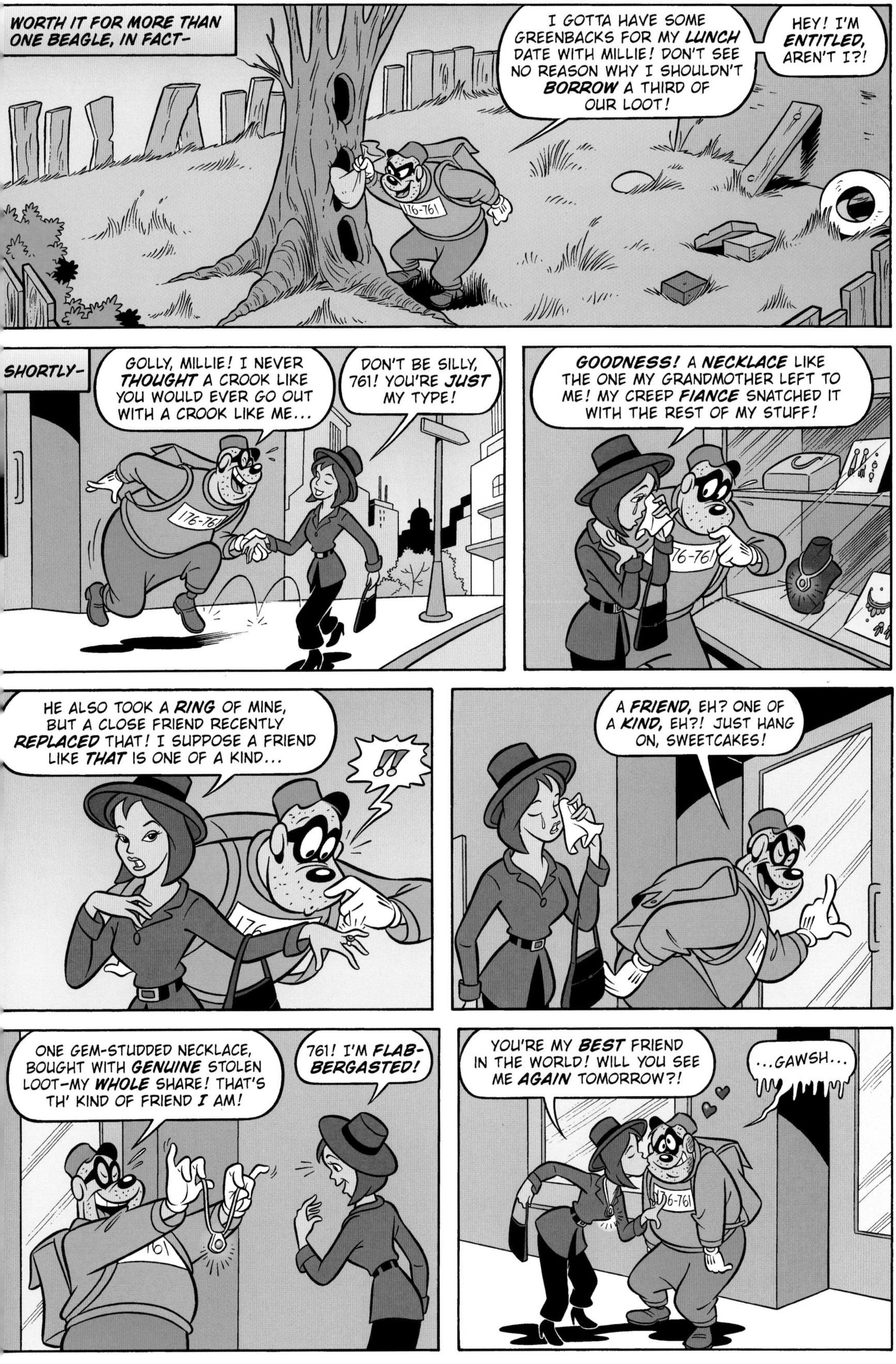
WORTH IT FOR MORE THAN ONE BEAGLE, IN FACT–
I GOTTA HAVE SOME GREENBACKS FOR MY LUNCH DATE WITH MILLIE! DON'T SEE NO REASON WHY I SHOULDN'T BORROW A THIRD OF OUR LOOT!
HEY! I'M ENTITLED, AREN'T I?!
176-761
SHORTLY–
GOLLY, MILLIE! I NEVER THOUGHT A CROOK LIKE YOU WOULD EVER GO OUT WITH A CROOK LIKE ME...
DON'T BE SILLY, 761! YOU'RE JUST MY TYPE!
176-761
GOODNESS! A NECKLACE LIKE THE ONE MY GRANDMOTHER LEFT TO ME! MY CREEP FIANCE SNATCHED IT WITH THE REST OF MY STUFF!
HE ALSO TOOK A RING OF MINE, BUT A CLOSE FRIEND RECENTLY REPLACED THAT! I SUPPOSE A FRIEND LIKE THAT IS ONE OF A KIND...
!!
A FRIEND, EH? ONE OF A KIND, EH?! JUST HANG ON, SWEETCAKES!
ONE GEM-STUDDED NECKLACE, BOUGHT WITH GENUINE STOLEN LOOT–MY WHOLE SHARE! THAT'S TH' KIND OF FRIEND I AM!
761! I'M FLABBERGASTED!
YOU'RE MY BEST FRIEND IN THE WORLD! WILL YOU SEE ME AGAIN TOMORROW?!
...GAWSH...
176-761

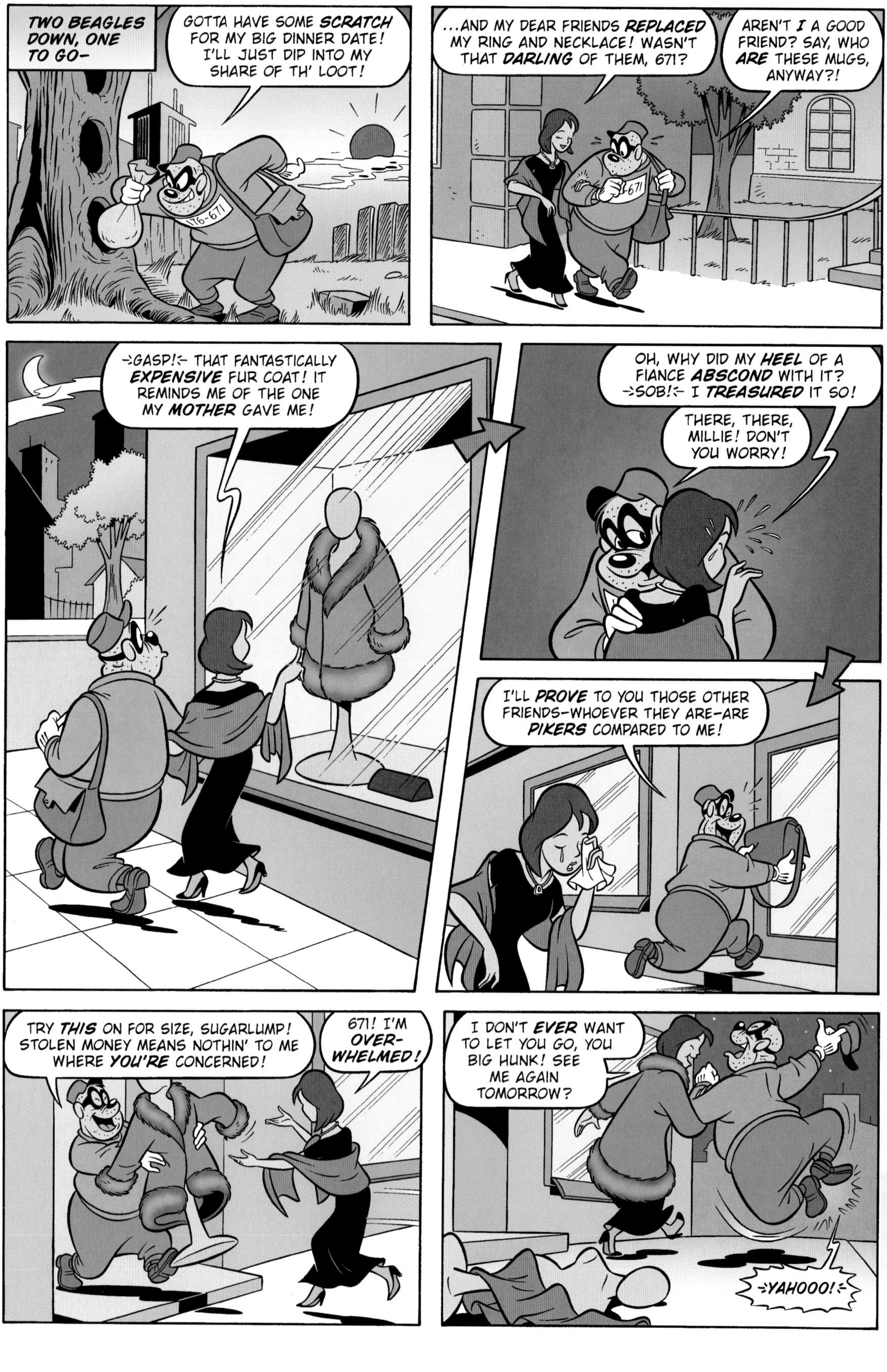
TWO BEAGLES DOWN, ONE TO GO–
GOTTA HAVE SOME SCRATCH FOR MY BIG DINNER DATE! I'LL JUST DIP INTO MY SHARE OF TH' LOOT!
176-671
...AND MY DEAR FRIENDS REPLACED MY RING AND NECKLACE! WASN'T THAT DARLING OF THEM, 671?
AREN'T I A GOOD FRIEND? SAY, WHO ARE THESE MUGS, ANYWAY?!
671
-GASP!- THAT FANTASTICALLY EXPENSIVE FUR COAT! IT REMINDS ME OF THE ONE MY MOTHER GAVE ME!
OH, WHY DID MY HEEL OF A FIANCE ABSCOND WITH IT? -SOB!- I TREASURED IT SO!
THERE, THERE, MILLIE! DON'T YOU WORRY!
I'LL PROVE TO YOU THOSE OTHER FRIENDS–WHOEVER THEY ARE–ARE PIKERS COMPARED TO ME!
TRY THIS ON FOR SIZE, SUGARLUMP! STOLEN MONEY MEANS NOTHIN' TO ME WHERE YOU'RE CONCERNED!
671! I'M OVER-WHELMED!
I DON'T EVER WANT TO LET YOU GO, YOU BIG HUNK! SEE ME AGAIN TOMORROW?
-YAHOOO!-

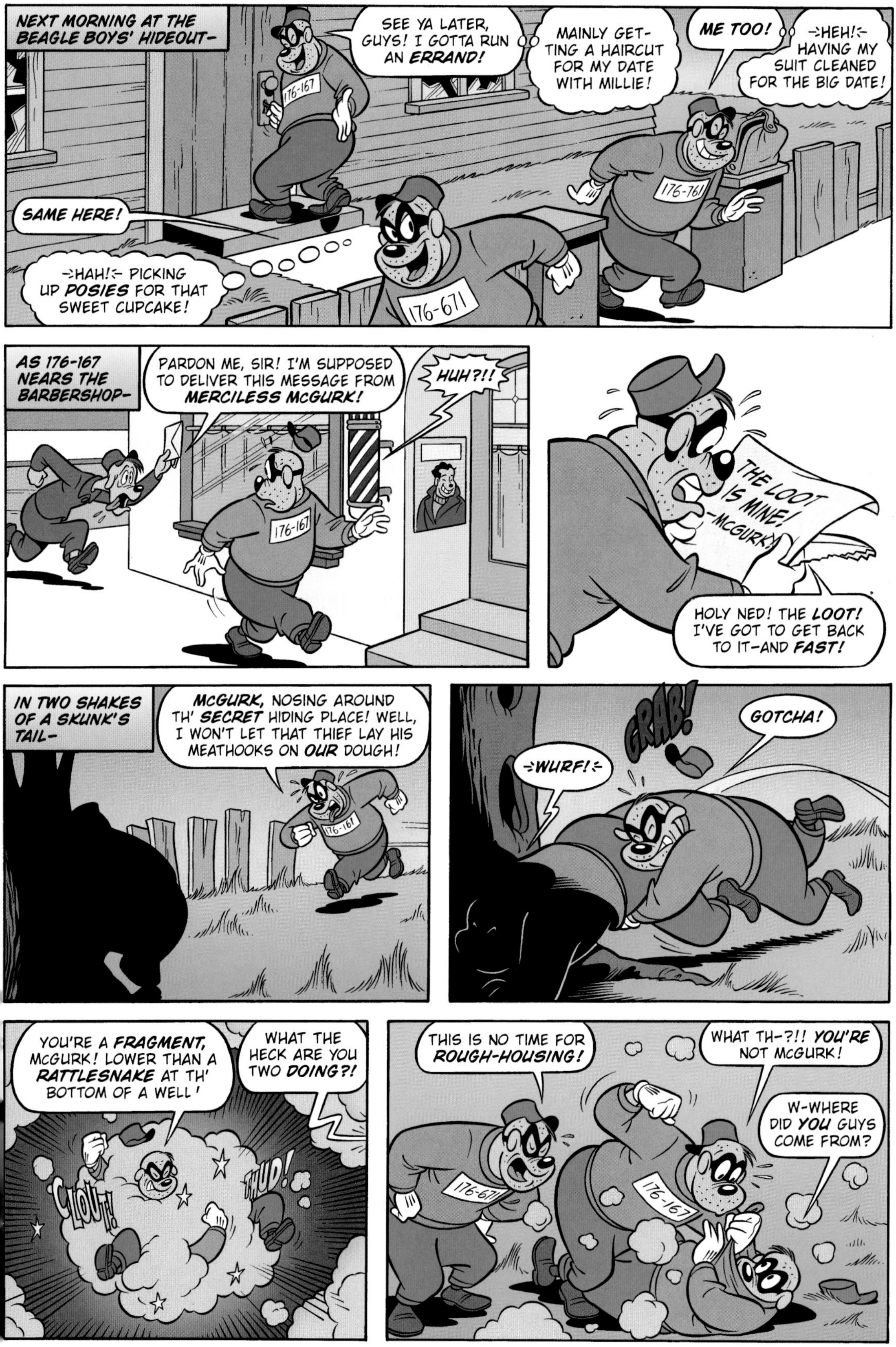
NEXT MORNING AT THE BEAGLE BOYS' HIDEOUT—
SEE YA LATER, GUYS! I GOTTA RUN AN ERRAND!
MAINLY GETTING A HAIRCUT FOR MY DATE WITH MILLIE!
ME TOO!
HEH! HAVING MY SUIT CLEANED FOR THE BIG DATE!
SAME HERE!
HAH! PICKING UP POSIES FOR THAT SWEET CUPCAKE!
176-167
176-761
176-671
AS 176-167 NEARS THE BARBERSHOP—
PARDON ME, SIR! I'M SUPPOSED TO DELIVER THIS MESSAGE FROM MERCILESS McGURK!
HUH?!!
THE LOOT IS MINE! —McGURK
HOLY NED! THE LOOT! I'VE GOT TO GET BACK TO IT—AND FAST!
IN TWO SHAKES OF A SKUNK'S TAIL—
McGURK, NOSING AROUND TH' SECRET HIDING PLACE! WELL, I WON'T LET THAT THIEF LAY HIS MEATHOOKS ON OUR DOUGH!
GRAB!
GOTCHA!
WURF!
YOU'RE A FRAGMENT, McGURK! LOWER THAN A RATTLESNAKE AT TH' BOTTOM OF A WELL!
WHAT THE HECK ARE YOU TWO DOING?!
CLOUT!
THUD!
THIS IS NO TIME FOR ROUGH-HOUSING!
WHAT TH-?!! YOU'RE NOT McGURK!
W-WHERE DID YOU GUYS COME FROM?

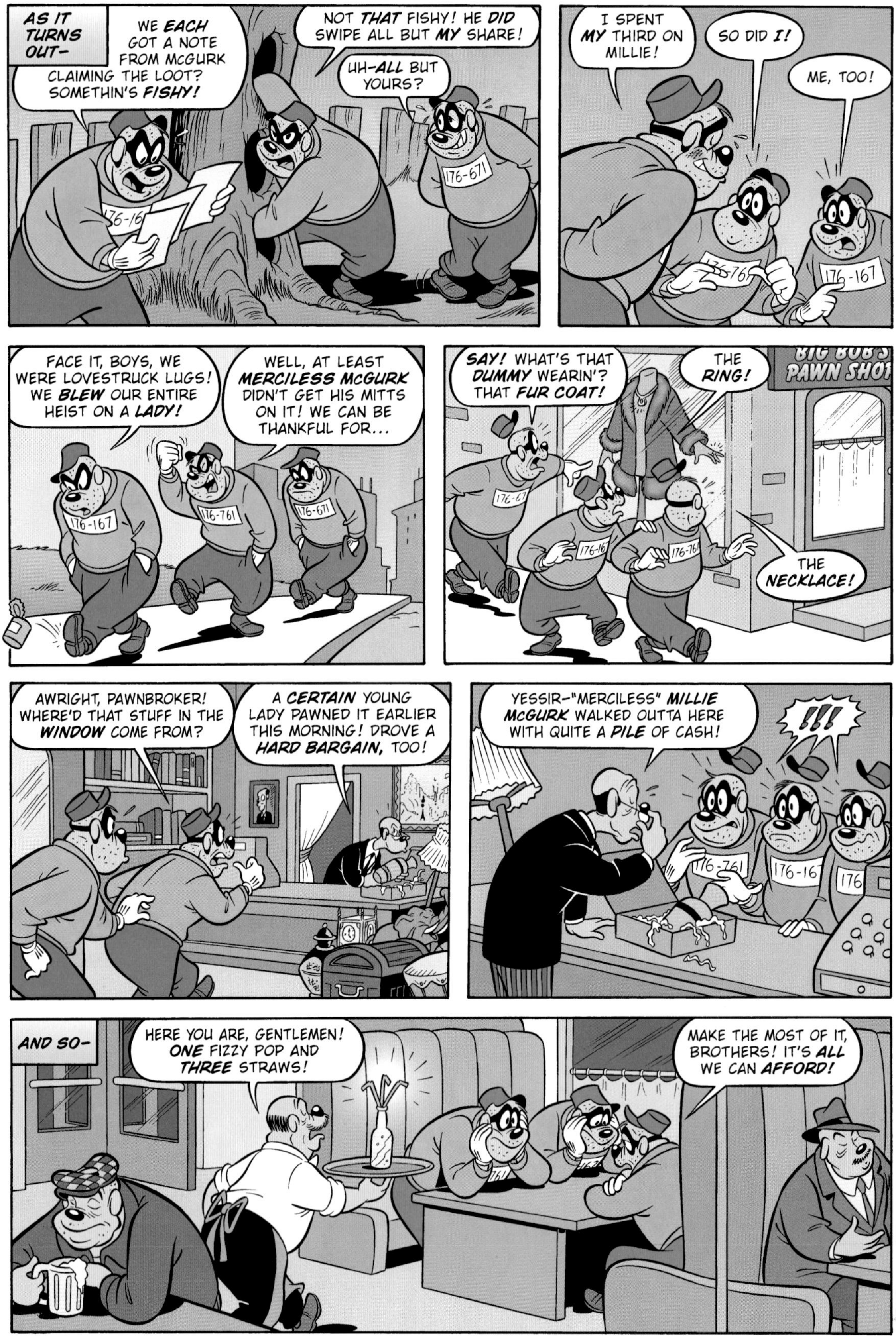
AS IT TURNS OUT—
WE EACH GOT A NOTE FROM McGURK CLAIMING THE LOOT? SOMETHIN'S FISHY!
NOT THAT FISHY! HE DID SWIPE ALL BUT MY SHARE!
UH-ALL BUT YOURS?
176-16
176-671
I SPENT MY THIRD ON MILLIE!
SO DID I!
ME, TOO!
176-761
176-167
FACE IT, BOYS, WE WERE LOVESTRUCK LUGS! WE BLEW OUR ENTIRE HEIST ON A LADY!
WELL, AT LEAST MERCILESS McGURK DIDN'T GET HIS MITTS ON IT! WE CAN BE THANKFUL FOR...
176-167
176-761
176-671
SAY! WHAT'S THAT DUMMY WEARIN'? THAT FUR COAT!
THE RING!
BIG BOB'S PAWN SHOP
THE NECKLACE!
AWRIGHT, PAWNBROKER! WHERE'D THAT STUFF IN THE WINDOW COME FROM?
A CERTAIN YOUNG LADY PAWNED IT EARLIER THIS MORNING! DROVE A HARD BARGAIN, TOO!
YESSIR—"MERCILESS" MILLIE McGURK WALKED OUTTA HERE WITH QUITE A PILE OF CASH!
!!!
AND SO—
HERE YOU ARE, GENTLEMEN! ONE FIZZY POP AND THREE STRAWS!
MAKE THE MOST OF IT, BROTHERS! IT'S ALL WE CAN AFFORD!

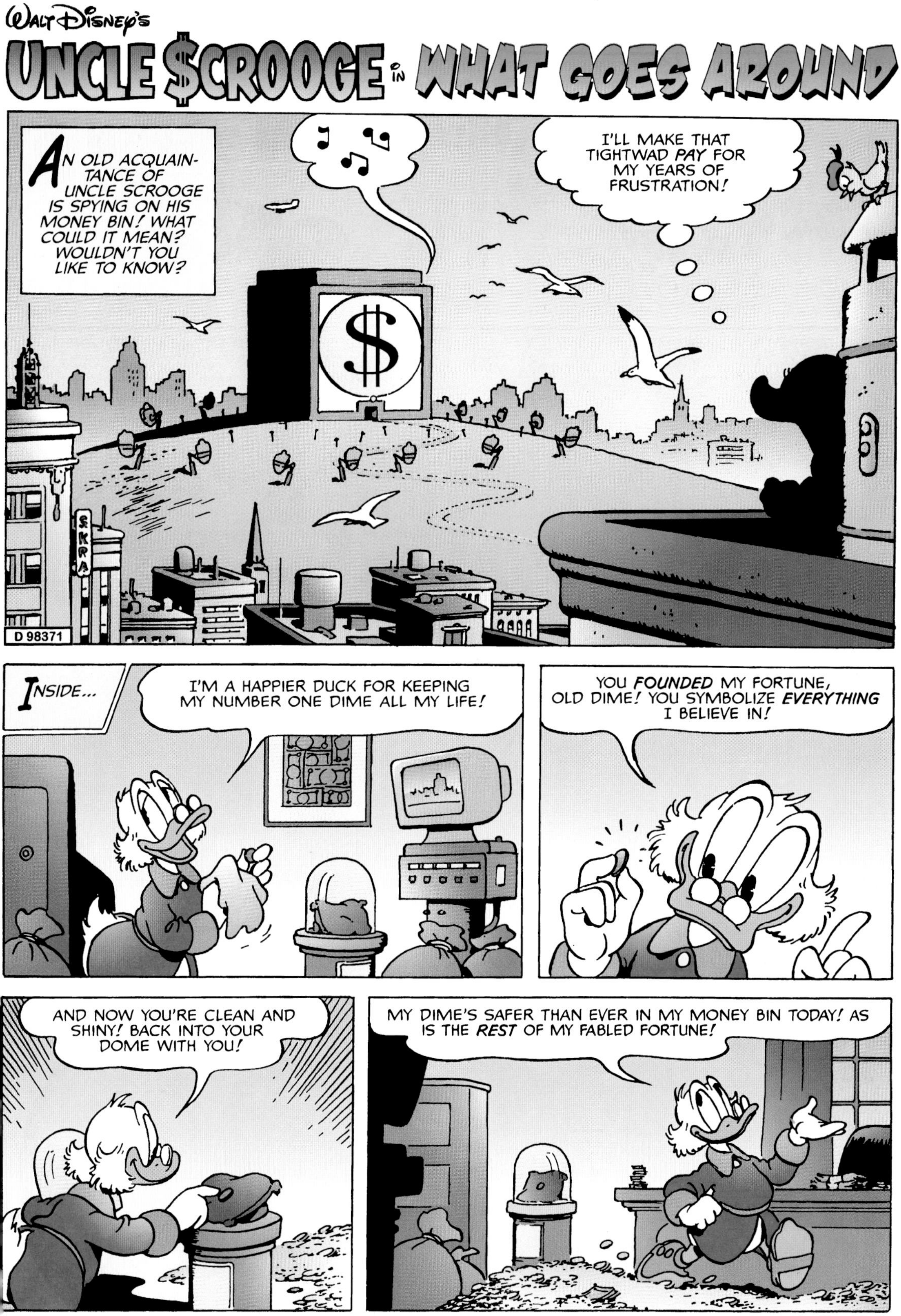
WALT DISNEY'S
UNCLE $CROOGE IN WHAT GOES AROUND
AN OLD ACQUAINTANCE OF UNCLE SCROOGE IS SPYING ON HIS MONEY BIN! WHAT COULD IT MEAN? WOULDN'T YOU LIKE TO KNOW?
I'LL MAKE THAT TIGHTWAD PAY FOR MY YEARS OF FRUSTRATION!
D 98371
INSIDE...
I'M A HAPPIER DUCK FOR KEEPING MY NUMBER ONE DIME ALL MY LIFE!
YOU FOUNDED MY FORTUNE, OLD DIME! YOU SYMBOLIZE EVERYTHING I BELIEVE IN!
AND NOW YOU'RE CLEAN AND SHINY! BACK INTO YOUR DOME WITH YOU!
MY DIME'S SAFER THAN EVER IN MY MONEY BIN TODAY! AS IS THE REST OF MY FABLED FORTUNE!

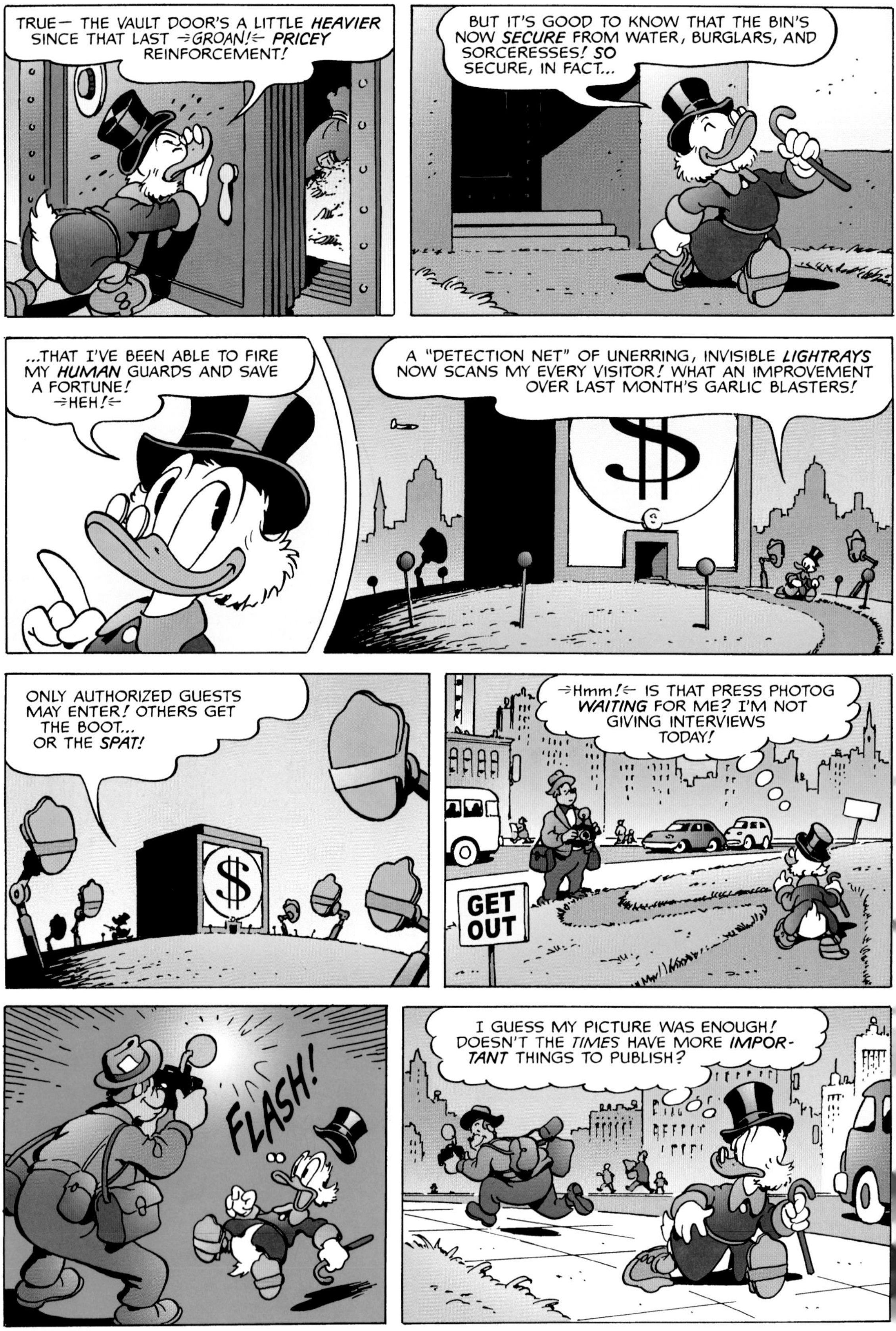
TRUE— THE VAULT DOOR'S A LITTLE HEAVIER SINCE THAT LAST ⇒GROAN!⇐ PRICEY REINFORCEMENT!
BUT IT'S GOOD TO KNOW THAT THE BIN'S NOW SECURE FROM WATER, BURGLARS, AND SORCERESSES! SO SECURE, IN FACT...
...THAT I'VE BEEN ABLE TO FIRE MY HUMAN GUARDS AND SAVE A FORTUNE! ⇒HEH!⇐
A "DETECTION NET" OF UNERRING, INVISIBLE LIGHTRAYS NOW SCANS MY EVERY VISITOR! WHAT AN IMPROVEMENT OVER LAST MONTH'S GARLIC BLASTERS!
ONLY AUTHORIZED GUESTS MAY ENTER! OTHERS GET THE BOOT... OR THE SPAT!
⇒Hmm!⇐ IS THAT PRESS PHOTOG WAITING FOR ME? I'M NOT GIVING INTERVIEWS TODAY!
GET OUT
FLASH!
I GUESS MY PICTURE WAS ENOUGH! DOESN'T THE TIMES HAVE MORE IMPORTANT THINGS TO PUBLISH?

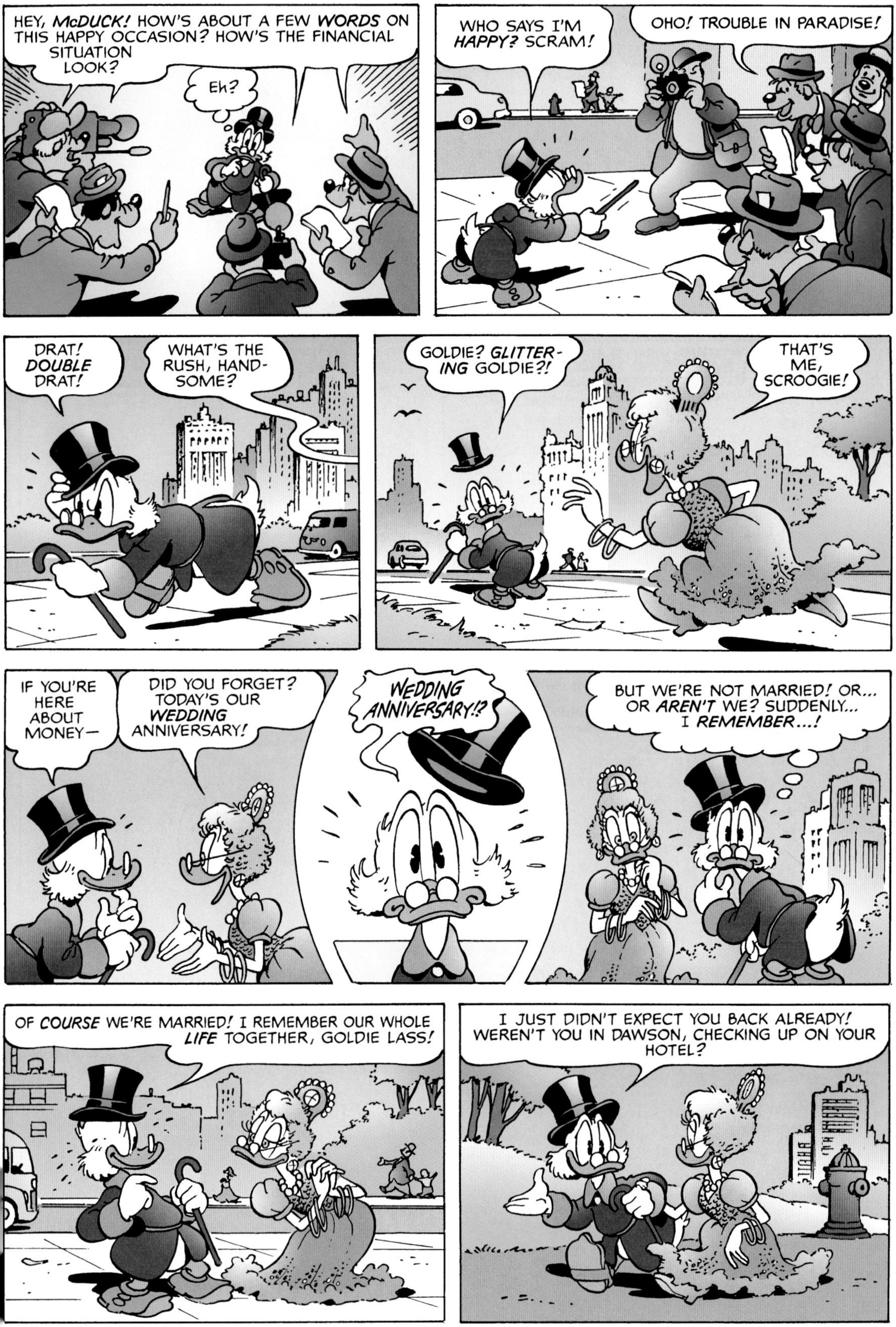
HEY, McDUCK! HOW'S ABOUT A FEW WORDS ON THIS HAPPY OCCASION? HOW'S THE FINANCIAL SITUATION LOOK?
Eh?
WHO SAYS I'M HAPPY? SCRAM!
OHO! TROUBLE IN PARADISE!
DRAT! DOUBLE DRAT!
WHAT'S THE RUSH, HANDSOME?
GOLDIE? GLITTERING GOLDIE?!
THAT'S ME, SCROOGIE!
IF YOU'RE HERE ABOUT MONEY—
DID YOU FORGET? TODAY'S OUR WEDDING ANNIVERSARY!
WEDDING ANNIVERSARY!?
BUT WE'RE NOT MARRIED! OR... OR AREN'T WE? SUDDENLY... I REMEMBER...!
OF COURSE WE'RE MARRIED! I REMEMBER OUR WHOLE LIFE TOGETHER, GOLDIE LASS!
I JUST DIDN'T EXPECT YOU BACK ALREADY! WEREN'T YOU IN DAWSON, CHECKING UP ON YOUR HOTEL?

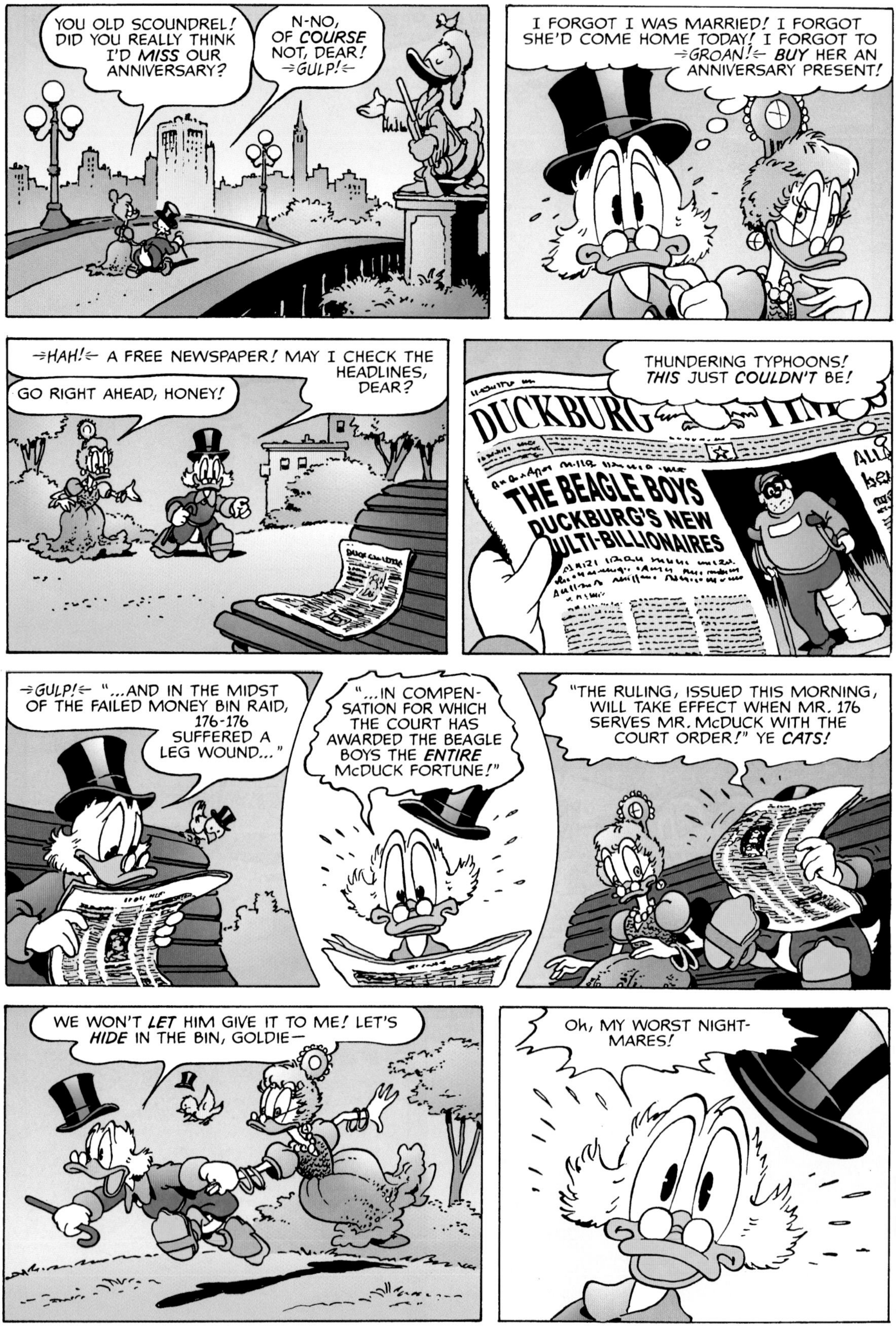
YOU OLD SCOUNDREL! DID YOU REALLY THINK I'D *MISS* OUR ANNIVERSARY?
N-NO, OF *COURSE* NOT, DEAR! ⇒GULP!⇐
I FORGOT I WAS MARRIED! I FORGOT SHE'D COME HOME TODAY! I FORGOT TO ⇒GROAN!⇐ *BUY* HER AN ANNIVERSARY PRESENT!
⇒HAH!⇐ A FREE NEWSPAPER! MAY I CHECK THE HEADLINES, DEAR?
GO RIGHT AHEAD, HONEY!
THUNDERING TYPHOONS! *THIS* JUST *COULDN'T* BE!
DUCKBURG
THE BEAGLE BOYS
DUCKBURG'S NEW
ULTI-BILLIONAIRES
⇒GULP!⇐ "...AND IN THE MIDST OF THE FAILED MONEY BIN RAID, 176-176 SUFFERED A LEG WOUND..."
"...IN COMPENSATION FOR WHICH THE COURT HAS AWARDED THE BEAGLE BOYS THE *ENTIRE* McDUCK FORTUNE!"
"THE RULING, ISSUED THIS MORNING, WILL TAKE EFFECT WHEN MR. 176 SERVES MR. McDUCK WITH THE COURT ORDER!" YE *CATS!*
WE WON'T *LET* HIM GIVE IT TO ME! LET'S *HIDE* IN THE BIN, GOLDIE—
Oh, MY WORST NIGHTMARES!

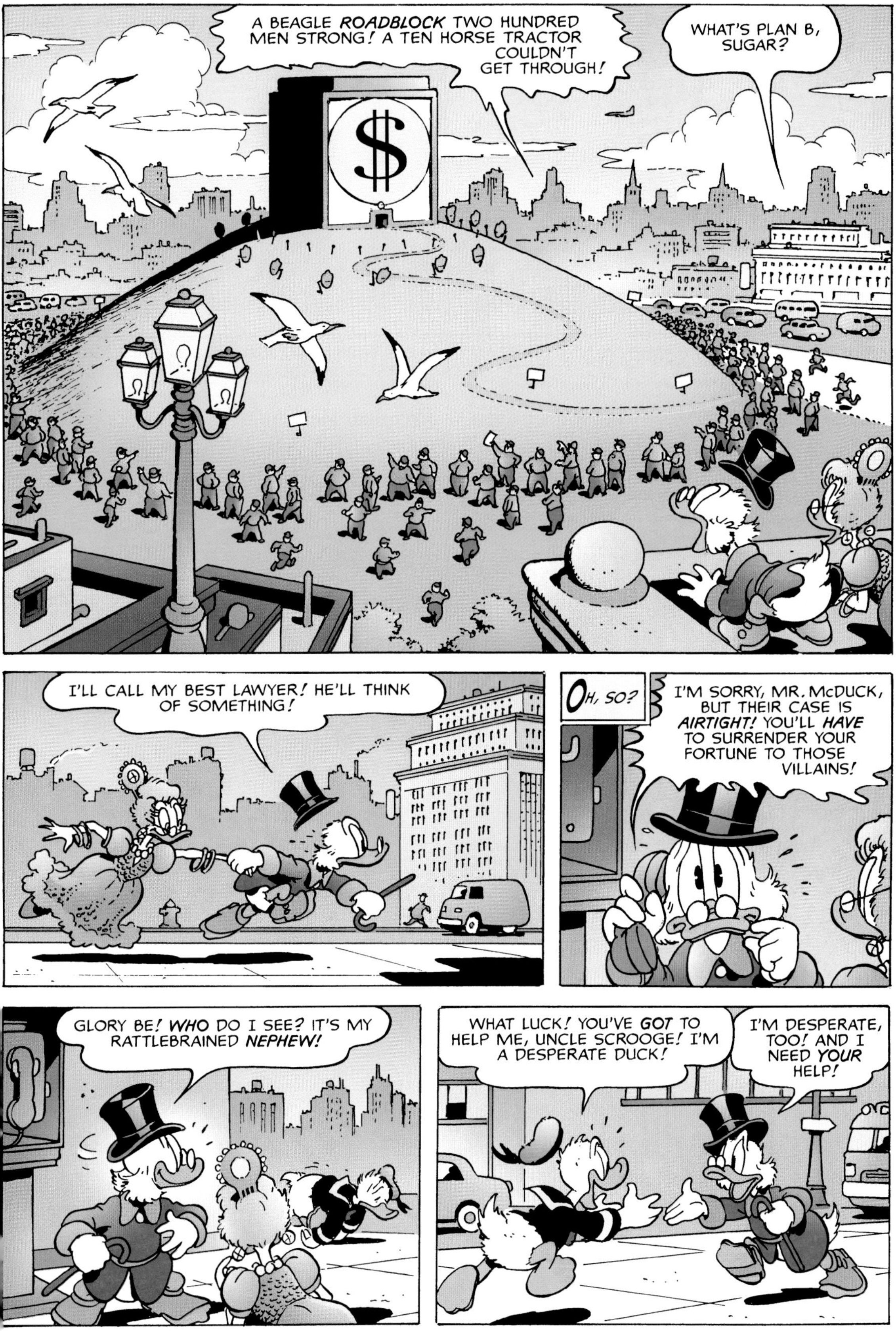
A BEAGLE ROADBLOCK TWO HUNDRED MEN STRONG! A TEN HORSE TRACTOR COULDN'T GET THROUGH!
WHAT'S PLAN B, SUGAR?
I'LL CALL MY BEST LAWYER! HE'LL THINK OF SOMETHING!
OH, SO?
I'M SORRY, MR. McDUCK, BUT THEIR CASE IS AIRTIGHT! YOU'LL HAVE TO SURRENDER YOUR FORTUNE TO THOSE VILLAINS!
GLORY BE! WHO DO I SEE? IT'S MY RATTLEBRAINED NEPHEW!
WHAT LUCK! YOU'VE GOT TO HELP ME, UNCLE SCROOGE! I'M A DESPERATE DUCK!
I'M DESPERATE, TOO! AND I NEED YOUR HELP!

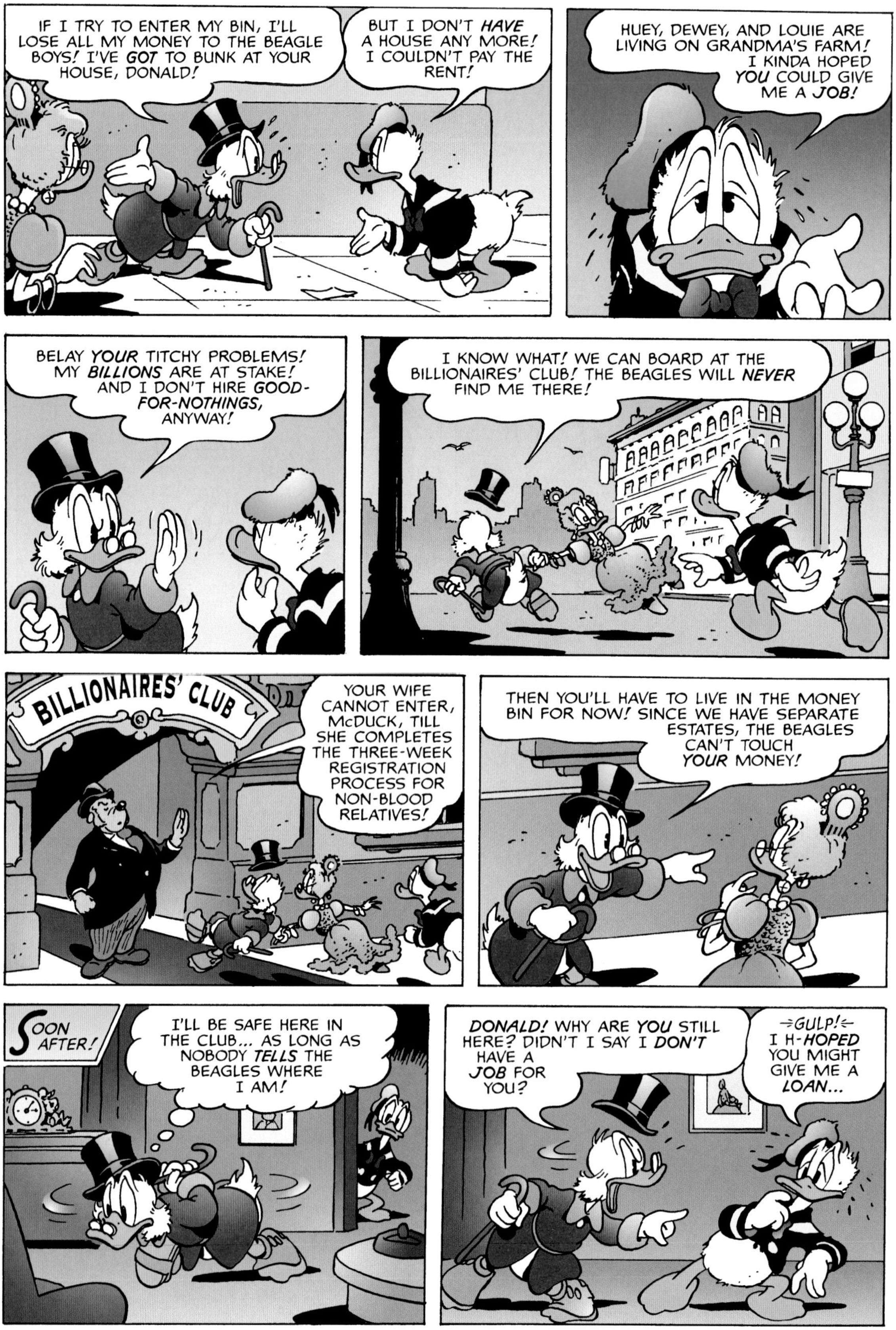
IF I TRY TO ENTER MY BIN, I'LL LOSE ALL MY MONEY TO THE BEAGLE BOYS! I'VE GOT TO BUNK AT YOUR HOUSE, DONALD!
BUT I DON'T HAVE A HOUSE ANY MORE! I COULDN'T PAY THE RENT!
HUEY, DEWEY, AND LOUIE ARE LIVING ON GRANDMA'S FARM! I KINDA HOPED YOU COULD GIVE ME A JOB!
BELAY YOUR TITCHY PROBLEMS! MY BILLIONS ARE AT STAKE! AND I DON'T HIRE GOOD-FOR-NOTHINGS, ANYWAY!
I KNOW WHAT! WE CAN BOARD AT THE BILLIONAIRES' CLUB! THE BEAGLES WILL NEVER FIND ME THERE!
BILLIONAIRES' CLUB
YOUR WIFE CANNOT ENTER, McDUCK, TILL SHE COMPLETES THE THREE-WEEK REGISTRATION PROCESS FOR NON-BLOOD RELATIVES!
THEN YOU'LL HAVE TO LIVE IN THE MONEY BIN FOR NOW! SINCE WE HAVE SEPARATE ESTATES, THE BEAGLES CAN'T TOUCH YOUR MONEY!
SOON AFTER!
I'LL BE SAFE HERE IN THE CLUB... AS LONG AS NOBODY TELLS THE BEAGLES WHERE I AM!
DONALD! WHY ARE YOU STILL HERE? DIDN'T I SAY I DON'T HAVE A JOB FOR YOU?
GULP! I H-HOPED YOU MIGHT GIVE ME A LOAN...

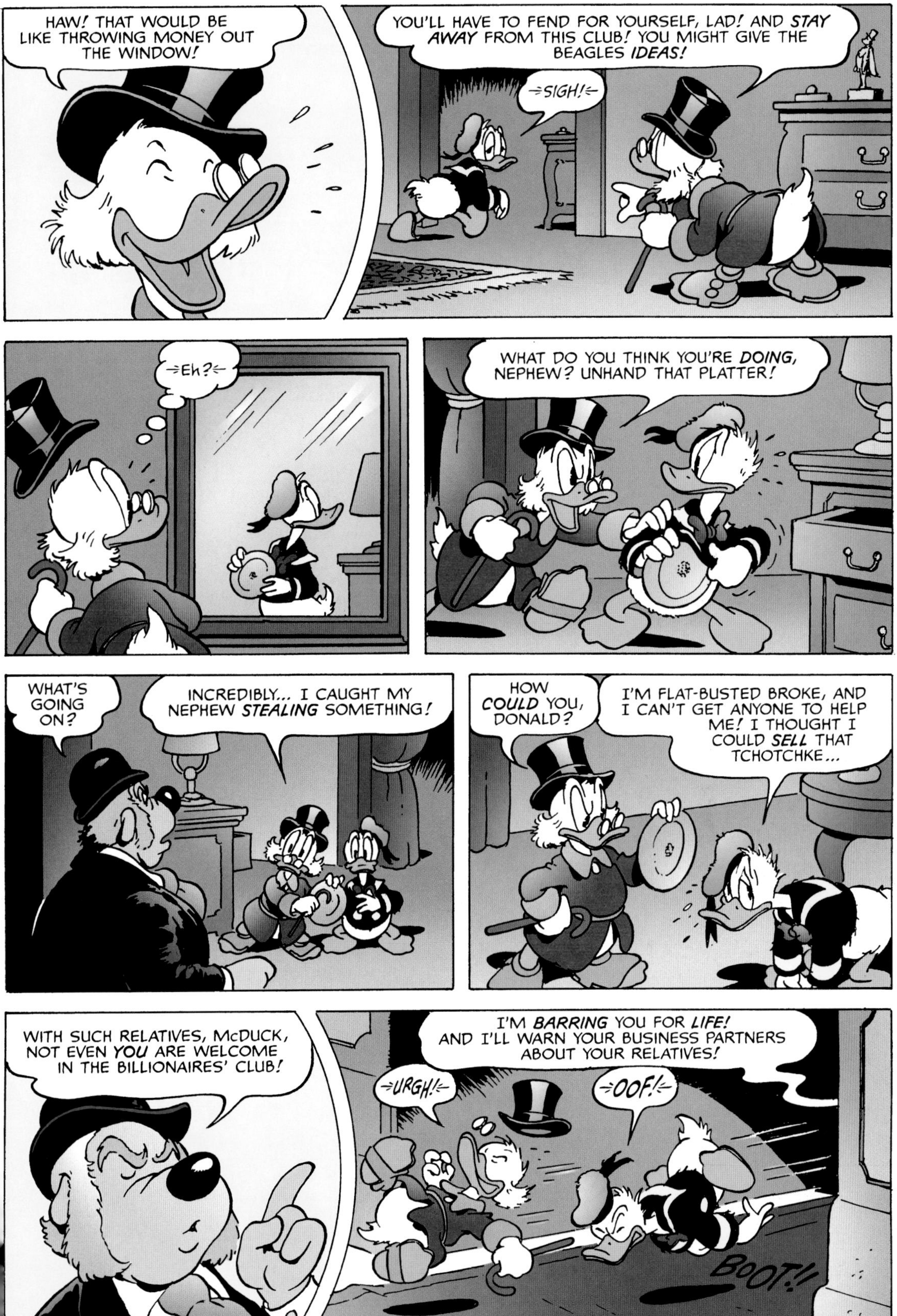
HAW! THAT WOULD BE LIKE THROWING MONEY OUT THE WINDOW!
YOU'LL HAVE TO FEND FOR YOURSELF, LAD! AND STAY AWAY FROM THIS CLUB! YOU MIGHT GIVE THE BEAGLES IDEAS!
SIGH!
Eh?
WHAT DO YOU THINK YOU'RE DOING, NEPHEW? UNHAND THAT PLATTER!
WHAT'S GOING ON?
INCREDIBLY... I CAUGHT MY NEPHEW STEALING SOMETHING!
HOW COULD YOU, DONALD?
I'M FLAT-BUSTED BROKE, AND I CAN'T GET ANYONE TO HELP ME! I THOUGHT I COULD SELL THAT TCHOTCHKE...
WITH SUCH RELATIVES, McDUCK, NOT EVEN YOU ARE WELCOME IN THE BILLIONAIRES' CLUB!
I'M BARRING YOU FOR LIFE! AND I'LL WARN YOUR BUSINESS PARTNERS ABOUT YOUR RELATIVES!
URGH!
OOF!
BOOT!!

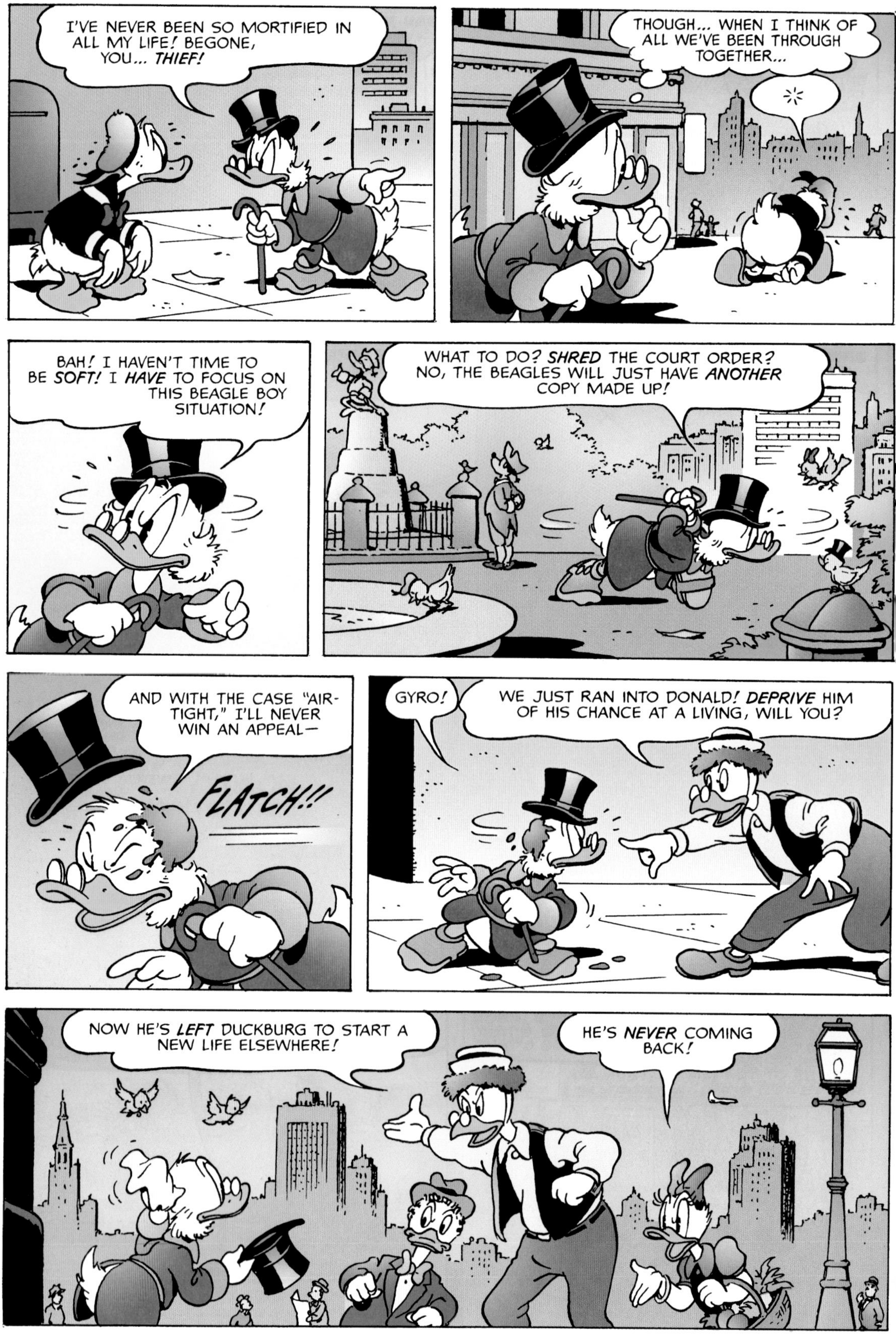
I'VE NEVER BEEN SO MORTIFIED IN ALL MY LIFE! BEGONE, YOU... THIEF!
THOUGH... WHEN I THINK OF ALL WE'VE BEEN THROUGH TOGETHER...
BAH! I HAVEN'T TIME TO BE SOFT! I HAVE TO FOCUS ON THIS BEAGLE BOY SITUATION!
WHAT TO DO? SHRED THE COURT ORDER? NO, THE BEAGLES WILL JUST HAVE ANOTHER COPY MADE UP!
AND WITH THE CASE "AIR-TIGHT," I'LL NEVER WIN AN APPEAL—
FLATCH!!
GYRO!
WE JUST RAN INTO DONALD! DEPRIVE HIM OF HIS CHANCE AT A LIVING, WILL YOU?
NOW HE'S LEFT DUCKBURG TO START A NEW LIFE ELSEWHERE!
HE'S NEVER COMING BACK!

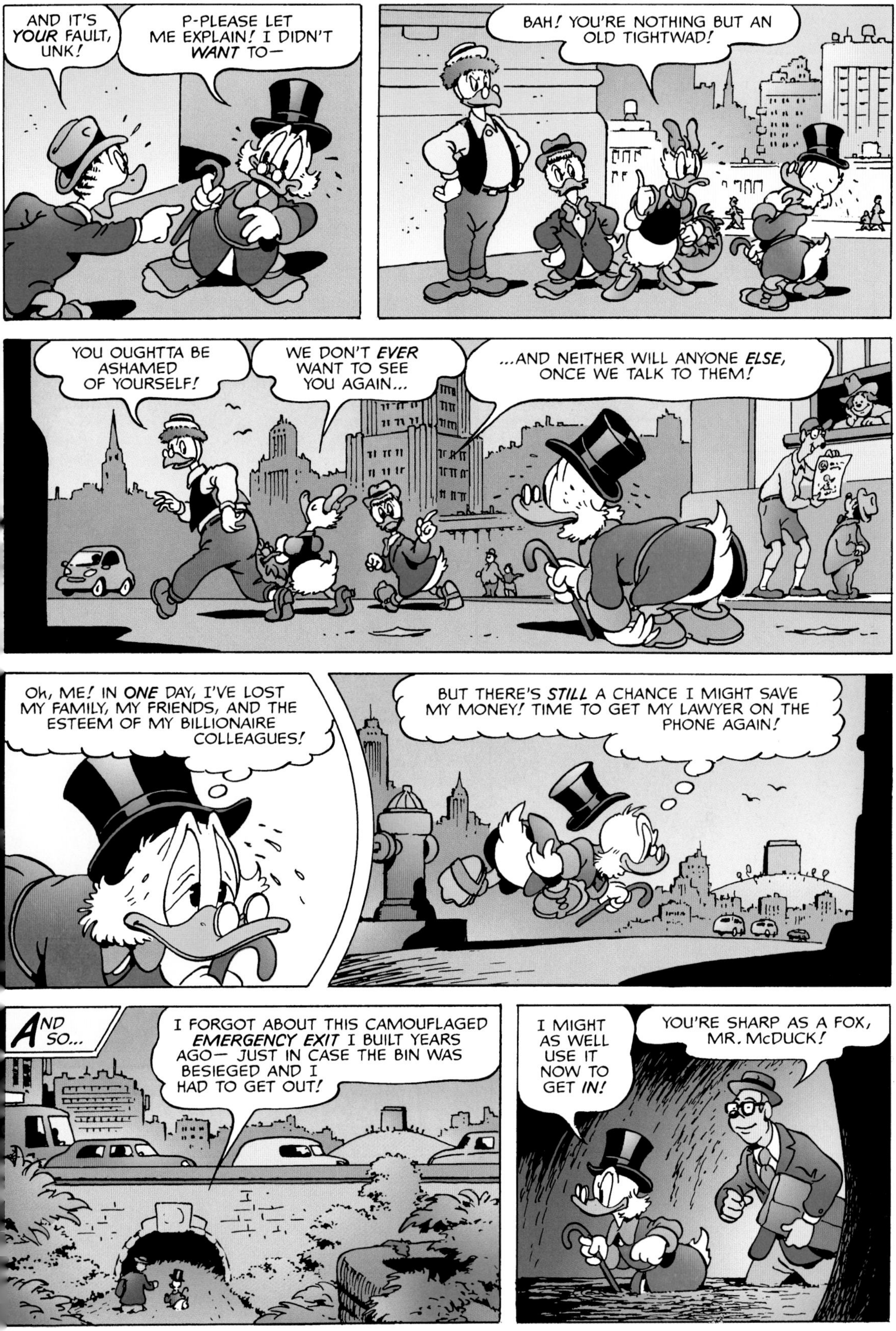

AND IT'S *YOUR* FAULT, UNK!
P-PLEASE LET ME EXPLAIN! I DIDN'T *WANT* TO—
BAH! YOU'RE NOTHING BUT AN OLD TIGHTWAD!
YOU OUGHTTA BE ASHAMED OF YOURSELF!
WE DON'T *EVER* WANT TO SEE YOU AGAIN...
...AND NEITHER WILL ANYONE *ELSE*, ONCE WE TALK TO THEM!
Oh, ME! IN *ONE* DAY, I'VE LOST MY FAMILY, MY FRIENDS, AND THE ESTEEM OF MY BILLIONAIRE COLLEAGUES!
BUT THERE'S *STILL* A CHANCE I MIGHT SAVE MY MONEY! TIME TO GET MY LAWYER ON THE PHONE AGAIN!
AND SO...
I FORGOT ABOUT THIS CAMOUFLAGED *EMERGENCY EXIT* I BUILT YEARS AGO— JUST IN CASE THE BIN WAS BESIEGED AND I HAD TO GET OUT!
I MIGHT AS WELL USE IT NOW TO GET *IN!*
YOU'RE SHARP AS A FOX, MR. McDUCK!

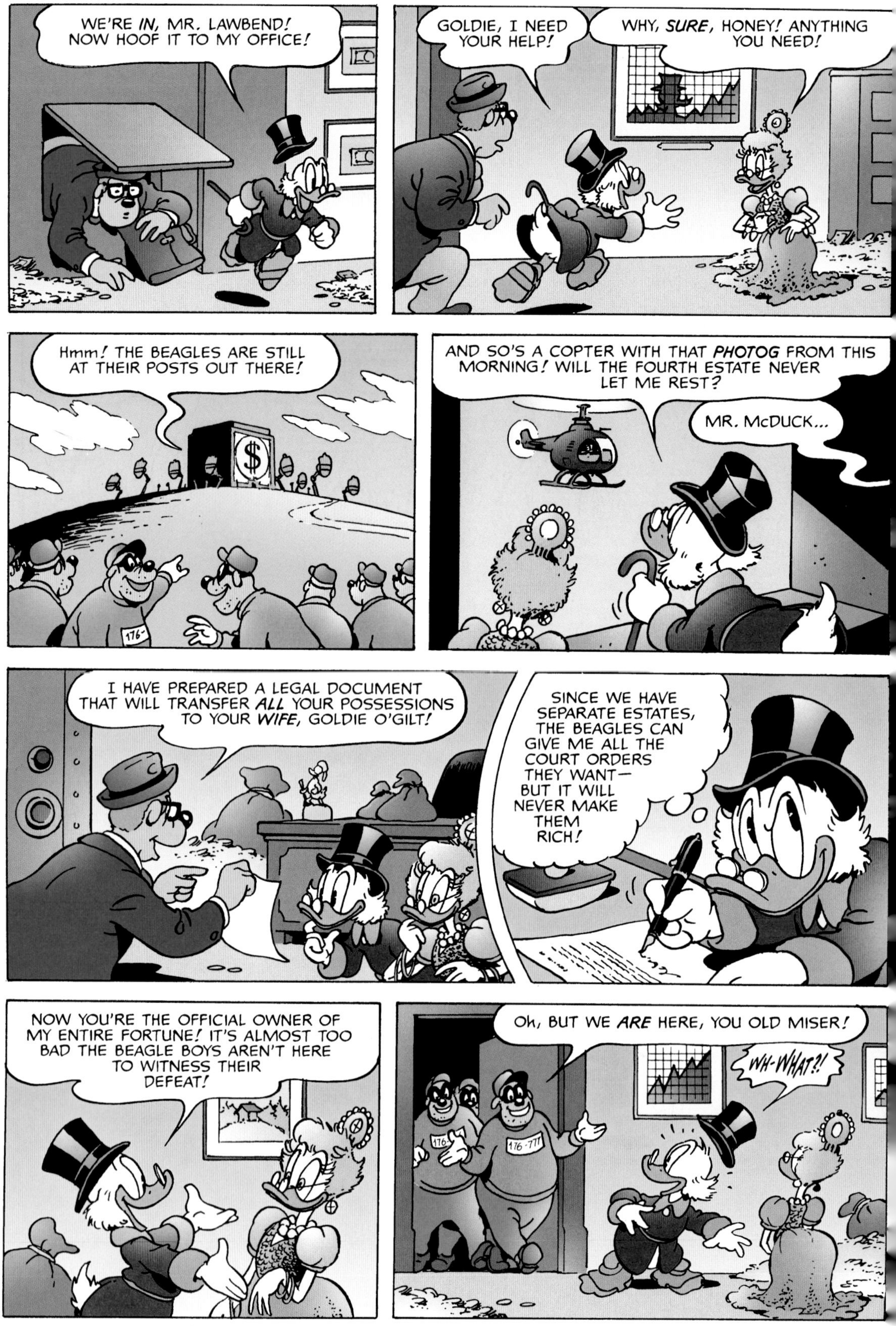
WE'RE IN, MR. LAWBEND! NOW HOOF IT TO MY OFFICE!
GOLDIE, I NEED YOUR HELP!
WHY, SURE, HONEY! ANYTHING YOU NEED!
Hmm! THE BEAGLES ARE STILL AT THEIR POSTS OUT THERE!
176-
AND SO'S A COPTER WITH THAT PHOTOG FROM THIS MORNING! WILL THE FOURTH ESTATE NEVER LET ME REST?
MR. McDUCK...
I HAVE PREPARED A LEGAL DOCUMENT THAT WILL TRANSFER ALL YOUR POSSESSIONS TO YOUR WIFE, GOLDIE O'GILT!
SINCE WE HAVE SEPARATE ESTATES, THE BEAGLES CAN GIVE ME ALL THE COURT ORDERS THEY WANT— BUT IT WILL NEVER MAKE THEM RICH!
NOW YOU'RE THE OFFICIAL OWNER OF MY ENTIRE FORTUNE! IT'S ALMOST TOO BAD THE BEAGLE BOYS AREN'T HERE TO WITNESS THEIR DEFEAT!
Oh, BUT WE ARE HERE, YOU OLD MISER!
WH-WHAT?!
176-
176-777

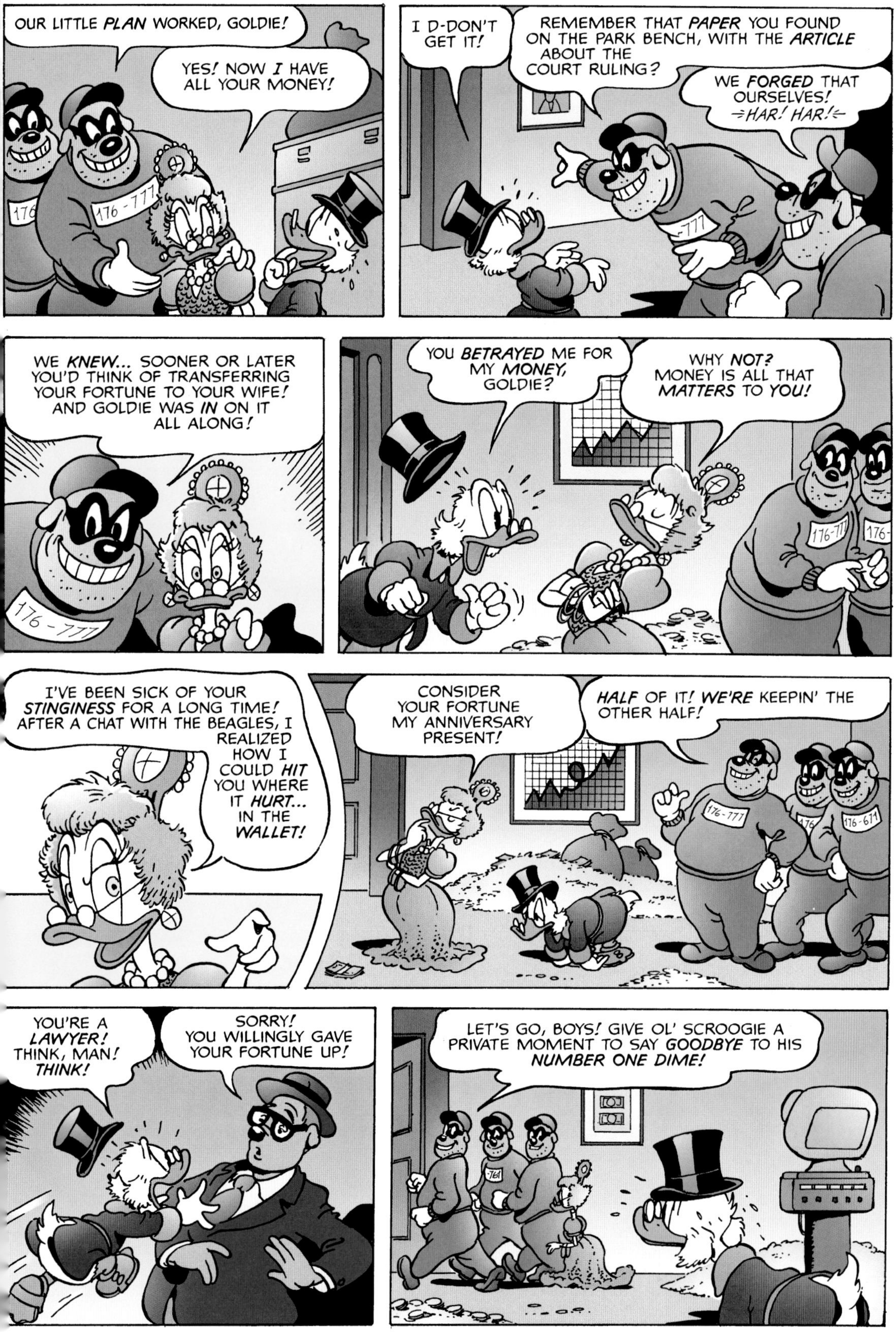
OUR LITTLE *PLAN* WORKED, GOLDIE!
YES! NOW *I* HAVE ALL YOUR MONEY!
I D-DON'T GET IT!
REMEMBER THAT *PAPER* YOU FOUND ON THE PARK BENCH, WITH THE *ARTICLE* ABOUT THE COURT RULING?
WE *FORGED* THAT OURSELVES! ⇒HAR! HAR!⇐
WE *KNEW...* SOONER OR LATER YOU'D THINK OF TRANSFERRING YOUR FORTUNE TO YOUR WIFE! AND GOLDIE WAS *IN* ON IT ALL ALONG!
YOU *BETRAYED* ME FOR MY *MONEY,* GOLDIE?
WHY *NOT?* MONEY IS ALL THAT *MATTERS* TO *YOU!*
I'VE BEEN SICK OF YOUR *STINGINESS* FOR A LONG TIME! AFTER A CHAT WITH THE BEAGLES, I REALIZED HOW I COULD *HIT* YOU WHERE IT *HURT...* IN THE *WALLET!*
CONSIDER YOUR FORTUNE MY ANNIVERSARY PRESENT!
HALF OF IT! *WE'RE* KEEPIN' THE OTHER HALF!
YOU'RE A *LAWYER!* THINK, MAN! *THINK!*
SORRY! YOU WILLINGLY GAVE YOUR FORTUNE UP!
LET'S GO, BOYS! GIVE OL' SCROOGIE A PRIVATE MOMENT TO SAY *GOODBYE* TO HIS *NUMBER ONE DIME!*

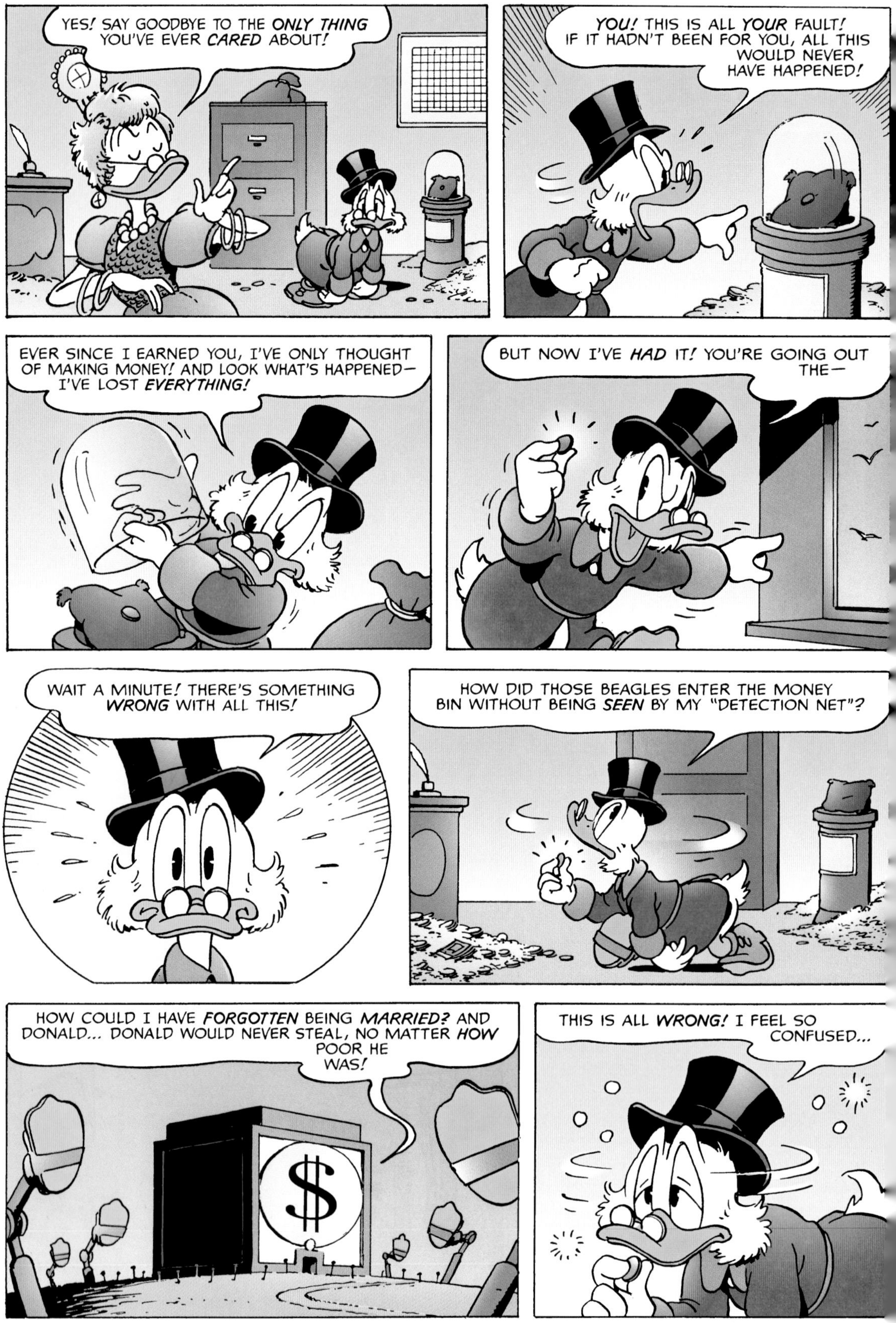
YES! SAY GOODBYE TO THE ONLY THING YOU'VE EVER CARED ABOUT!
YOU! THIS IS ALL YOUR FAULT! IF IT HADN'T BEEN FOR YOU, ALL THIS WOULD NEVER HAVE HAPPENED!
EVER SINCE I EARNED YOU, I'VE ONLY THOUGHT OF MAKING MONEY! AND LOOK WHAT'S HAPPENED— I'VE LOST EVERYTHING!
BUT NOW I'VE HAD IT! YOU'RE GOING OUT THE—
WAIT A MINUTE! THERE'S SOMETHING WRONG WITH ALL THIS!
HOW DID THOSE BEAGLES ENTER THE MONEY BIN WITHOUT BEING SEEN BY MY "DETECTION NET"?
HOW COULD I HAVE FORGOTTEN BEING MARRIED? AND DONALD... DONALD WOULD NEVER STEAL, NO MATTER HOW POOR HE WAS!
$
THIS IS ALL WRONG! I FEEL SO CONFUSED...

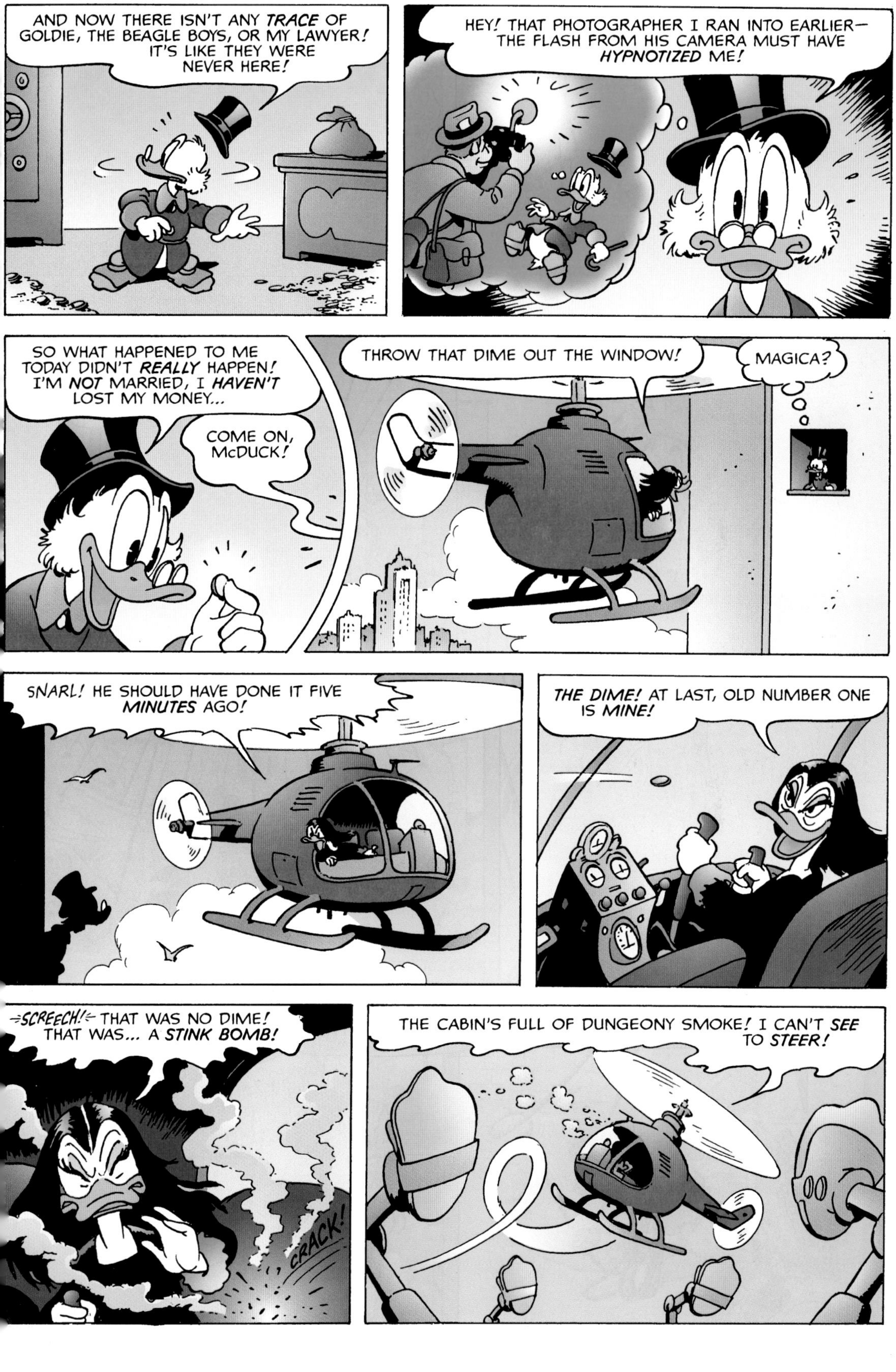
AND NOW THERE ISN'T ANY TRACE OF GOLDIE, THE BEAGLE BOYS, OR MY LAWYER! IT'S LIKE THEY WERE NEVER HERE!
HEY! THAT PHOTOGRAPHER I RAN INTO EARLIER— THE FLASH FROM HIS CAMERA MUST HAVE HYPNOTIZED ME!
SO WHAT HAPPENED TO ME TODAY DIDN'T REALLY HAPPEN! I'M NOT MARRIED, I HAVEN'T LOST MY MONEY...
COME ON, McDUCK!
THROW THAT DIME OUT THE WINDOW!
MAGICA?
SNARL! HE SHOULD HAVE DONE IT FIVE MINUTES AGO!
THE DIME! AT LAST, OLD NUMBER ONE IS MINE!
SCREECH! THAT WAS NO DIME! THAT WAS... A STINK BOMB!
CRACK!
THE CABIN'S FULL OF DUNGEONY SMOKE! I CAN'T SEE TO STEER!

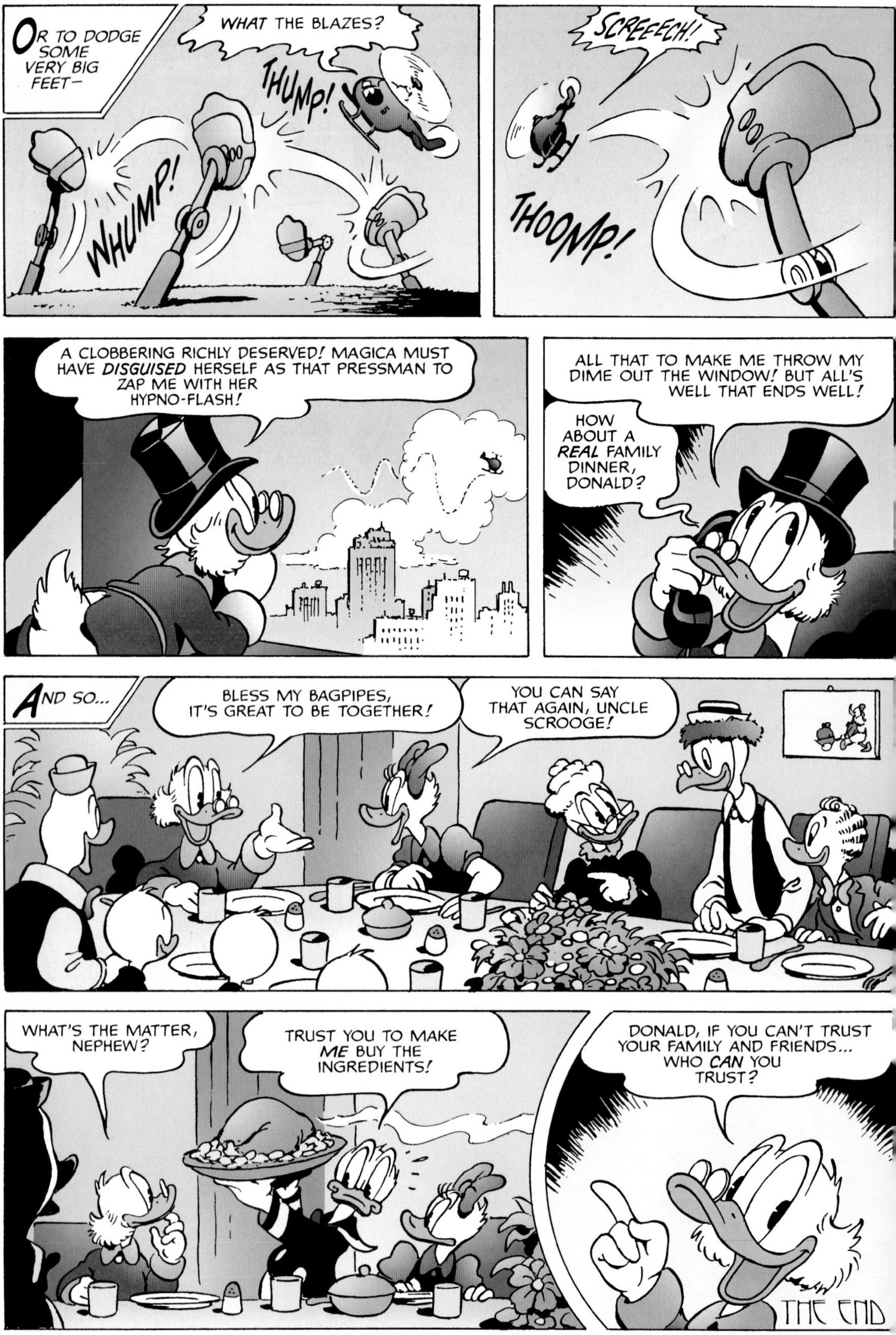
OR TO DODGE SOME VERY BIG FEET—
WHAT THE BLAZES?
THUMP!
WHUMP!
SCREEECH!
THOOMP!
A CLOBBERING RICHLY DESERVED! MAGICA MUST HAVE DISGUISED HERSELF AS THAT PRESSMAN TO ZAP ME WITH HER HYPNO-FLASH!
ALL THAT TO MAKE ME THROW MY DIME OUT THE WINDOW! BUT ALL'S WELL THAT ENDS WELL!
HOW ABOUT A REAL FAMILY DINNER, DONALD?
AND SO...
BLESS MY BAGPIPES, IT'S GREAT TO BE TOGETHER!
YOU CAN SAY THAT AGAIN, UNCLE SCROOGE!
WHAT'S THE MATTER, NEPHEW?
TRUST YOU TO MAKE ME BUY THE INGREDIENTS!
DONALD, IF YOU CAN'T TRUST YOUR FAMILY AND FRIENDS... WHO CAN YOU TRUST?
THE END